CHAPTER ONE

Caroline cleared her throat imperiously. 'I think it's time Robert found himself a wife – you must take him to London, Wyckeham.'

Jason Warwycke, fourth Marquess of Wyckeham, slowly completed his perusal of the *Gazette* and looked up at his sister-in-law, who was seated at the opposite end of the polished dining table. It was long enough to seat ten people either side, but at this moment, Jason would have been happier if it had been twice that length.

'Is that so?' he replied. Although his tone was even, there was an underlying sarcasm that anyone but Caroline would have noticed. As always, however, she was entirely oblivious to anything other than having her way.

'Well, he needs some town bronze, so you

may as well kill two birds with one stone, don't you think? It surely can't be good for him to spend all his time here in the country.'

Jason stifled a sigh and put down his paper. It was obvious that there would be no peace in which to read until Caroline had left the room. 'As far as I am aware, Robert has not expressed any desire either to go to London or to take a wife. He seems perfectly happy to stay where he is.'

Robert Warwycke was his nephew, the son of his late brother Gerald, who had been killed in a hunting accident some five years previously. As Gerald had left his wife and son in dire straits financially, Jason had invited them to live with him. It had suited him to have them in his house so that he could keep an eye on the boy, now that he was his guardian, and he was pleased with the way his nephew had turned out, despite having to fight Caroline every step of the way with regard to his education and upbringing.

At Robert's coming of age a few months previously, however, Jason had judged it time that the young man learned to fend for himself. He had bought him a small country estate to run, and Robert had thrown himself into this task with enthusiasm. They had hardly seen him since, and Jason doubted very much whether he could be tempted away any time soon.

'Pah! He won't find a wife in deepest Wiltshire.' Caroline made it sound as remote as Outer Mongolia and Jason stifled a sardonic smile; she had been born and bred in that very county herself, and that was where Gerald had found her.

'He's very close to Bath, you know. Plenty of society there,' he murmured, but she ignored the interruption and continued as if he hadn't spoken.

'There are no families of any note in those parts, none at all. No, you must take him to London and soon, before he falls in love with some unsuitable country girl, not fit to be the next Marchioness of Wyckeham.'

A spurt of anger, so strong it surprised him, shot through Jason at Caroline's blithe assumption that he himself would never beget any heirs, and that it was a foregone conclusion that Robert would be the next marquess. Jason was only thirty-two, for heaven's sake, not in his dotage, and even though he had declared to all and sundry that he would never wed again, there was no reason why he couldn't change his mind.

Granted, his first foray into the married state had been a disaster, and he had sworn not to repeat that mistake, but he thought there may come a time when he felt differently. Caroline was taking too much for granted. He clenched his jaw in determination and came to a swift decision. Now that Robert no longer lived at Wyckeham Hall, there was really no need for Caroline to remain either. As the only woman in the household, he had given her leave to run things as she saw fit with the help of his housekeeper, never quibbling about any expense, however vast. During the last year, however, he had noted several instances of downright mistreatment of his servants and he felt the time had come for him to put his foot down. She was becoming insufferable and she had to go.

Making a mental note to speak to his steward about having the Dower House refurbished as quickly as possible, so that Caroline could be moved there, he turned his thoughts back to her initial demand – that he take Rob to London to find a bride. Although the boy may not be ready for such a big step as yet, perhaps it wasn't such a bad idea to take him to the capital for some town bronze, as she had suggested. As his closest relative and possible future marquess (he emphasised the word 'possible' in his thoughts with another unconscious clenching of his jaw), Rob could not be allowed to turn into too much of a country bumpkin.

'Very well, I will take him to London,' he said after thinking it over for a moment longer. 'I have to go there on a business matter anyway, but don't expect any miracles. At that age, he's bound to fall in love with someone unsuitable no matter where he is, take my word for it.'

And I should know, he thought to himself. He hadn't listened to any warnings about his own marriage, had thought himself grown up and in control. He sighed inwardly once more. He would just have to make sure Robert was prevented from making the same mistake, forcibly if necessary. That kind of union he wouldn't wish on his worst enemy.

CHAPTER TWO

A sharp voice interrupted the young girl's reverie. 'Ianthe, why do you not make yourself useful for a change and fetch us some lemonade instead of propping up that pillar. Upon my word, you look very ill-bred lounging like that.'

Ianthe Templeton dragged her gaze away from the dance floor, and frowned in her mother's direction, but the latter had already turned away, secure in the knowledge that her daughter would do her bidding. After all, it wasn't as if she had anything else to do, since no one was asking her to dance. Trying valiantly not to scowl, Ianthe made her way towards the refreshment table set up in a room adjoining the ballroom, tamping down thoughts of rebellion. It may be a singular honour to have been given vouchers for

Almack's, but she for one would rather have stayed at home with a good book.

She sighed, collected two glasses of the weak lemonade that tasted of nothing so much as dishwater, and returned to her mother. 'Here you are, Mama, the patronesses' idea of refreshment, as you requested.'

'Don't be impertinent, I'm sure it's perfectly adequate. You may hold on to Serena's until she has finished dancing with Lord Somerville.'

Lady Templeton barely glanced at Ianthe. Her eyes were focused on the dance floor, where Ianthe's twin sister, a young lady of exceptional beauty, was partnering the most eligible bachelor in the room, the Earl of Somerville. It was a sight to gladden any fond mama's heart, but this one in particular, thought Ianthe somewhat uncharitably. She knew that Lady Templeton wanted her daughters married into the highest echelons of society, and at present there was no one higher than his lordship currently available on the marriage mart. The fact that he was also handsome, albeit in a rather flamboyant way, merely added to his considerable charm.

Ianthe suppressed another sigh. For herself, she would have been happy to receive an offer from any eligible gentleman, so long as he promised to take her away from London and the mindless entertainments offered there, but since no one was even asking her to dance, this did not seem a very likely scenario. Early on in the season she had acquired a reputation as a blue-stocking, having unwisely mentioned a book on philosophy she had been reading to a young man whose only interests were horses and fisticuffs. The gossips had picked up on this morsel with glee. Since she and Serena were not identical twins, she didn't even have her sister's good looks with which to mitigate such a deplorable tendency, and from that moment on her chances of making a good match had shrunk to almost none.

She wondered for the umpteenth time why her mother had even brought her to Almack's. The patronesses had only included Ianthe in their invitation as an afterthought; it was clear it was Serena they really wanted, since she was the current belle of the season.

The dance came to an end and Serena was escorted ceremoniously back to her mama by the Earl.

'I shall procure you some lemonade, Miss Templeton,' he announced, and Ianthe's protest was cut short by a quelling look from her mother.

'How very kind. I'm sure that dear Serena must be exceedingly thirsty after all that dancing.'

Ianthe turned away in order to hide her moue of distaste at her parent's simpering. She knew she ought not to criticise, but her mother was so transparent. If it wasn't for the fact that Serena was so lovely, no doubt the Earl would have fled long before now. After all, who would want to be saddled with someone like Lady Templeton for a mother-in-law?

To pass the time, Ianthe took a sip of the

lemonade that was now hers and almost spat it out again. Not only did it taste awful, but it was lukewarm into the bargain. Surreptitiously, she placed the glass on the floor behind a large pot plant and returned to lean on the pillar once more.

Serena had now been joined by two of her best friends, and the trio were awaiting Lord Somerville's return with much giggling and fluttering of fans, when suddenly a collective gasp went through the crowded room and a momentary hush fell. All eyes turned to the door, where two latecomers had only just made it through the hallowed portals before the cut-off time of eleven o'clock. No one, not even the Prince Regent himself, would have been allowed in after that time.

The doors swung shut behind them and the older of the two men stopped to survey the crowd with a sardonic lift of one eyebrow. Fierce whispering broke out on all sides, but he ignored it and bowed to the patroness on duty that evening, Lady Sally Jersey, obviously introducing the young man to her.

'Who is that, Mama?' Serenea whispered, uttering the question that had been hovering on Ianthe's tongue. 'He looks … dangerous.'

Lady Templeton gave a little shudder. 'Indeed, and so he should. It is none other than the Marquess of Wyckeham. Lord Wicked, they call him, because he murdered his wife. I am surprised he dares to show his face here.'

Serena gasped, but one of her companions was made of sterner stuff. 'Surely that was never proven, Lady Templeton, and he wasn't charged with anything. Didn't she fall down the stairs? An unfortunate accident, I was told.'

'Pushed, more likely,' her ladyship sniffed. 'It was a well-known fact that they didn't get along and when she couldn't produce the requisite heir…' She left the sentence hanging ominously, waiting for her young audience to draw their own conclusion.

'Really, Mama, you shouldn't repeat such

gossip. Someone might hear you,' Ianthe protested, but she found herself intrigued nonetheless.

Staring at the Marquess from across the room, she could well understand why people might think him capable of murder. With his sharp features and dressed all in black, apart from a snowy cravat tied in an intricate pattern, he did indeed look formidable and his clothes merely served to accentuate the excellent physique and hidden strength that so obviously lay underneath. The man exuded a latent power, like a big cat waiting to pounce, but as his gaze swept the room and briefly connected with hers, Ianthe glimpsed fierce intelligence and lazy amusement, rather than any menace. Her mother had to be wrong, she decided.

'I'll thank you to keep your advice to yourself, young lady,' Lady Templeton grumbled. 'I know what I know, and you'll not convince me otherwise. And stop lounging, for heaven's sakes. It's no wonder no one's dancing with you, you look like nothing so much as a hay sack.'

Ianthe gritted her teeth and turned away to hide her anger. If only she could escape – but there were still six weeks of the season to go and her mother and sister were determined to remain until the very end.

'Shh, Mama, they're coming this way,' Serena hissed, and composed her features, fixing a small smile on her face to show off the dimples either side of her mouth. 'Whatever he did, he's a marquess, which is higher than an earl, isn't it?' Her mother nodded. 'Well, then, who cares what he's done?'

Ianthe disapproved strongly of such a calculated way of looking at a man. To overlook his peccadilloes simply because of his exalted rank seemed to her the outside of enough.

But who was she to judge? She would never get the chance to choose between a marquess and an earl, so it didn't matter one jot to her. Still, she couldn't suppress an urge to look at the man again. He fascinated her. Perhaps he was a magician instead of a murderer? She stifled a gurgle of laughter at her own silliness. Really, she must stop reading Gothic tales; they were putting strange thoughts into her head.

Jason waited patiently while Lady Jersey interrogated his nephew as to his prospects, intentions and general likes and dislikes. Robert was a kind young man and replied as best he could, but when he shot his uncle a glance that was a distinct plea for help, Jason deemed it time to intervene.

'Sally, my dear, do stop chattering and perform your duty by introducing Robert to some suitable dancing partners. Do you see anyone that you fancy the look of in particular, Rob?' he asked his nephew.

Robert scanned the crowd, as did Jason, and by coincidence their eyes alighted on the same group of women, seated in the centre of the one wall. 'That dark beauty over there, is she spoken for?'

Lady Jersey craned her neck to follow his

gaze. 'Well, as good as, but you never know your luck. That's the Templeton chit, or chits I should say. There's two of them, but only one worth having. Not a penny to her name, but a diamond of the first water. She's got the Earl of Somerville eating out of her hand.'

'You said there were two?' Jason prompted, his gaze on quite a different lady, one who did not appear to be enjoying the evening's entertainment at all, which was unusual for someone so young.

'What? Oh, yes, she has a twin sister. Not identical in any respect, a blue-stocking by all accounts. Equally poor, so no point courting her either unless you like bookish females, which you didn't, last I heard.' Lady Jersey chuckled to herself and Jason swallowed a sharp retort. She must be referring to his last mistress, who had been incredibly beautiful but as dim as they came. Jason doubted if Alice even knew how to read. Perhaps that was part of the reason why he had lost interest in her so quickly and had finished their association some months earlier.

'Will you introduce us to the Templetons, please?' he asked curtly.

'By all means, follow me.'

Lady Jersey set off through the throng, which parted just as the Red Sea had done for Moses. Jason hid a smile at this sight, marvelling at the power of Almack's patronesses. No one wished to antagonise them in any way, lest they were barred from attending.

The crowd had no such scruples when it came to himself, he noticed. Jason watched with secret amusement as several people glared at him and whispered to their friends, as if they resented the presence amongst them of a man reputed to be a murderer. Others stared openly, obviously trying to decide whether he might be guilty or not. He barely glanced at them; let them believe what they wished. He hadn't murdered Elizabeth – though, the Lord knew, he'd wanted to often enough – and didn't give a fig what others thought. These people could go to the devil for all he cared.

The clusters of people shifted and he spied again the young lady who had caught his eye earlier. She was still leaning against a pillar, her arms crossed under her bosom, which was shapely enough, but not as ample as that of the dark beauty seated next to her. As he continued to walk towards them, he glanced at the so-called 'diamond of the first water' for a moment, in order to compare the two further. They both had dark hair, so black it was almost blue, but whereas the beauty had had hers fashioned into an intricate coiffure, the girl by the pillar wore a simple topknot which seemed to be coming undone since there were wisps of hair falling down either side of her face.

Both had large blue eyes fringed by long sooty lashes, but there the similarities ended. The prettier one had a tiny retroussé nose and a rosebud mouth framed by dimples; the other girl's nose was long and aquiline, her mouth more generous with only a hint of a dimple on one side. As Jason registered the smile fixed on the beauty's rosy lips, however, he realised how utterly false it was, and with an imperceptible shake of his head he returned his gaze to his original quarry, the girl by the pillar.

Lady Jersey stopped in front of the party. 'Ladies, may I introduce Lord Wyckeham and his nephew Mr Robert Warwycke. Gentlemen, this is Lady Templeton, Miss Serena Templeton, Miss Ianthe Templeton and the Misses Sarah and Anne Gardiner.'

Everyone bowed or curtseyed as required, and Lady Jersey engaged Lady Templeton in a brief conversation while Robert bowed over the elder Miss Templeton's hand and asked for a dance. She glanced at Jason, as if hoping to entice him onto the floor with her first, but when he pretended not to notice and remained silent, she replied, 'Well, I do believe my card is full, sir, but perhaps I could ask one of my partners to allow you to cut in.' With an imperious finger, she beckoned some hapless youth who had been hovering nearby, waiting for his dance.

'Osterly, you wouldn't mind missing a dance with me, would you?'

It wasn't really a question, and she didn't bother to wait for the poor gentleman's reply before standing up and placing her hand on Robert's arm. 'Shall we?' She flashed her dimples at him and at Jason, adding an extra flutter of her eyelashes at the latter, then swept onto the dance floor. Jason understood immediately that she was only dancing with Robert in order to further her acquaintance with a marquess, and he sighed inwardly. By the look in Robert's eyes, he had fallen hard and fast, but without a title he would have no luck with the likes of Miss Serena Templeton. It would all end in tears. How very tiresome, to be sure.

Rob would be much better off with the other sister, Jason thought – obviously not one of the usual simpering misses, she would no doubt make an excellent wife. He decided to try and steer his nephew her way once Miss Serena dashed his hopes, which hopefully shouldn't take too long.

He turned his attention away from the dancing couple and glanced again at the sister. Miss Ianthe was taller and she was wearing a most ill-fitting dress; it looked as though she had thrown on whatever had come out of her wardrobe first. It was only because the material was slightly diaphanous and she was standing with light behind her that he could make out her true shape, which was very pleasing. Without such help, she would have looked a complete dowd, but she was no such thing, he realised.

Turning to her, instead of the two Misses Gardiner who had been waiting for him to choose one of them, he bowed and said courteously, 'May I have this dance, Miss Ianthe?'

She blinked in surprise, her eyebrows rising a fraction, but she remained calm and he thought he saw an expression of regret flit across her features.

'With me? Oh, I am sorry, my lord, but unlike my sister, I'm afraid I have not been granted permission to dance the waltz. I am sure there are other ladies who would be glad to oblige you.' She glanced pointedly at the two seated girls, but Jason ignored this.

Catching the eye of the patroness, who had by now moved on to gossip with someone else, he crooked his finger and Lady Jersey immediately made her way back to him. Several people watched this in open-mouthed surprise, the stout Lady Templeton included. Jason reflected that they didn't know Sally the way he did – her curiosity alone would have made her do his bidding in this instance as no doubt she scented a juicy piece of gossip.

'My lord? she enquired, sounding slightly breathless with anticipation.

'Apologies for interrupting your no doubt scintillating conversation with Lord Albemarle, but I would be vastly obliged if you could give Miss Ianthe permission to waltz with me?'

'But of course.' Lady Jersey nodded to them both, a speculative glance in her eyes, then turned away with a smile.

He held out his arm to Miss Ianthe, and without a word, she placed her hand on top of it. He swept her into the dance with effortless grace, despite the fact that it was a while since he had last performed it. He knew himself to be a good dancer, and was pleasantly surprised when Miss Ianthe matched his steps without too much trouble.

'You dance well,' he commented. 'Is this not your first time?'

'Yes, but I have only to follow you. It seems simple enough.'

He didn't tell her that many ladies found that beyond their capabilities and his toes had suffered accordingly on several occasions. Instead, he enjoyed the feel of her in his arms as he twirled her expertly around. There was only the smallest of contacts between them, where his hand held hers and the other rested lightly on her back, but it was considered very risqué and for the first time he understood why. Despite the minimal friction, he was surprised to find that he was extremely aware of her as a woman and judging by her heightened colour, she was experiencing similar feelings of acute awareness. In fact, there was a veritable electric current between them that he simply couldn't ignore.

This thought made him almost falter in his steps. What was this? He had only danced with her in order to further his nephew's suit. He wasn't supposed to be attracted to her himself. He shook himself mentally and took a deep breath. He didn't want a wife, and certainly not a chit only just out of the school room. It simply wouldn't do.

But his body was telling him otherwise.

Damnation.

Ianthe endeavoured to breathe normally, but found it increasingly difficult with Lord Wyckeham so near. A strange energy seemed to be passing through his fingertips into hers and snaking its way up her arm, and although she tried not to look at him, her gaze was drawn to his time and again. He had brown eyes, she noticed, but they were such a light brown, it was almost like looking through clear honey, which was very disconcerting.

'Are you enjoying this, Miss Ianthe?' he asked abruptly.

'Yes, very much so, my lord.'

'You are not afraid of me?'

His question took her by surprise, but she didn't hesitate to reply.

'No – should I be?'

She realised that she wasn't afraid of him in the slightest, at least not in the way he meant. The way his touch made her feel was another matter altogether and much more frightening than the silly rumours about him being a murderer.

He nodded, as if that short exchange took care of his supposed misdeeds, and changed the subject. 'I take it you had not done much dancing previously this evening?'

She smiled ruefully. 'Not any evening, my lord. I am seldom asked.'

His eyebrows lifted again, in that haughty

manner she had found fascinating from the very first moment of seeing him. 'And why is that, Miss Ianthe? You are not plain, nor suffering from a squint.'

She laughed, and stated matter-of-factly, 'Blue-stockings are not usually singled out for attention, my lord, with or without a squint. I have no idea why you chose to do so, but I am grateful for the opportunity to dance the waltz this once. It's heavenly.'

'Twice,' he corrected.

'I beg your pardon?'

'We will stand up for two dances. It would be impolite otherwise.'

'Oh, would it?'

Confusion swirled through her and she couldn't help but wonder what game he was playing. Asking her to dance once was strange enough, but twice? Everyone was sure to remark upon it, even though it was permitted. She glanced in Serena's direction and immediately wished that she had not. Her sister, although smiling at her beau, Mr Warwycke, managed to shoot a dagger look in Ianthe's direction which did not bode well. Serena's temper tantrums were legendary in the Templeton household and Ianthe was fairly certain they were to be treated to one later on. She decided to forget the prospect for now, and resolutely put it out of her mind. She was determined to enjoy every moment of this dance; she would not allow Serena and her foul moods to ruin it for her.

'May I ask why the patronesses allowed you to come to Almack's if they had no intention of persuading young men to dance with you?' Lord Wyckeham was inquiring with amusement.

'I believe Lady Jersey insisted I should come along just to spite my mother. They … do not get on. One of the other patronesses granted vouchers to my sister Serena, but Lady Jersey sent one for me too with a note saying they couldn't very well ask my sister and not me since we are twins. Naturally Mama couldn't refuse to bring me, even though she knew it was a waste of time.

Lady Jersey did try to persuade a few of the young men to dance with me the first time but they were already promised elsewhere.'

He frowned. 'I'm surprised Sally would put up with that.'

'She is not always here, and I think once she had forced Mama to bring me, she lost interest in the game.'

'I see.' They danced the second dance in silence, and Ianthe wondered whether perhaps she had said too much, but when Lord Wyckeham led her back to her mother, he seemed unruffled. He bowed over her hand and she thanked him for the dances.

'Not at all, the pleasure was mine.'

And with that, he turned on his heel and left the room.

'Well, I never!' Lady Templeton stared after him, perplexed. 'What was all that about?' She looked her younger daughter up and down. 'Were you ogling him, Ianthe?'

'Me? I wasn't even looking at him,' Ianthe protested, although that wasn't strictly true of course.

'You must have offended him then.'

'No, I don't believe so.'

Mr Warwycke, who had by now returned with Serena and overheard their remarks, tried to smooth things over. 'You mustn't mind my uncle,' he said with a smile. 'He is a strange fellow and never does what one expects him to. I'm sure he didn't mean to upset anyone. It's just his way.'

Neither Serena nor her mother looked convinced however, and as soon as Mr War-wycke had left them to dance with one of the Misses Gardiner, Serena hissed at Ianthe, 'You must have done something to chase him away. We'll speak about it later.' Then she was sailing off to dance once more with the Earl of Somerville.

Ianthe sighed and returned to her pillar. To her surprise, however, she wasn't left to prop it up for long. It seemed that the young men in the room had been galvanised into action by Lord Wyckeham's interest and everyone suddenly wanted to dance with her. She marvelled at their fickleness and thought to herself that they were nothing but a flock of sheep, going only where someone else led. Still, it was a vast improvement on being bored silly, so she resolved to herself not to complain.

By the time they reached home in the early hours of the morning, Serena was incandescent with rage at her sister's surprising success, but Ianthe was too tired to care.

'You'd better keep your hands off the Earl,' was Serene's morning greeting to her sister the following day. 'And don't even think of setting your cap at the Marquess. Not that he'd have you, as he's apparently sworn never to marry again, but I might try and see if I can change his mind.'

Ianthe looked up from her breakfast, trying not to let Serena rile her. She knew that if she rose to her bait, open warfare would ensue. 'I'm not interested in the Earl,' she replied evenly, ignoring the last part of Serena's sentence.

Her sister shot her a dark look, as if she

didn't believe this for a moment. 'I should hope not, because…'

She was interrupted by a knock on the door which heralded the arrival of a couple of housemaids carrying two vases of flowers each, followed by a footman with another bouquet.

'These arrived for the young ladies,' one of them said with a curtsey. 'Mr Balfour said to bring them in straight away.'

Inathe was astonished to find that two were for her and gazed in wonder at the gorgeous bouquets. No one had ever sent flowers to her before. The larger one consisted entirely of enormous red roses interspersed with greenery, while the slightly smaller one was made up of a mixture of pink and yellow blooms. Serena's bouquets were identical, and when Ianthe inspected the cards that accompanied the flowers, she found that one had been signed simply with a large W, while the other read 'R Warwycke'. Wyckeham and his nephew. A frisson went through her and she glanced up to find her sister looking daggers at her once again.

Serena came over and snatched the cards out of Ianthe's hand. 'This is intolerable,' she snarled. 'Why are they bothering to send flowers to you?'

Ianthe was about to reply, but her mother forestalled her. 'Now, now, Serena, they are merely showing us that they are polite young men. They are new in town and since they have only just made our acquaintance, they're not to know that you are usually the only recipient of floral tributes.

'Perhaps they thought to get in our good graces by buying bouquets for both of you? You are twins, after all. And look, you have a lovely bouquet here from the Earl as well, Ianthe doesn't.'

Serena mulled this over and flounced back to her seat, where she picked absently at a piece of toast. 'You may be right, but I'll not have Ianthe ruining things for me.' She turned to her sister and fixed her with a glare. 'At the musical soiree tonight, you'd better stay out of the way or else. It's not as if you have any interest in marrying, anyway.'

'And what if I have?' Ianthe asked, goaded into anger at last.

'Then find your own suitors; don't poach on my territory.'

'Girls, girls, really, this is most unseemly,' Lady Templeton admonished, but Serena paid her no need and merely swept out of the room without a backward glance. Ianthe was left to glare after her, more angry with herself for becoming entangled in the argument than with her sister for being so horrid.

'I hope she marries soon, so that the rest of the household might enjoy some peace,' she muttered.

'Oh, but she is doing awfully well, you know,' her mother commented mildly. 'The young men seem to flock to her side, but then you didn't do too badly yourself last night. Whatever the Marquess's faults, he certainly did you a favour by dancing with you. You must try to capitalise on that tonight, and do your utmost to encourage those gentlemen who danced with you yesterday.'

'Oh, Mama, *must* I go? I do so hate musical soirees. A lot of screeching, if you ask me. I'd far rather stay at home.'

'Have you taken leave of your senses? Now that you've finally managed to attract some attention, you can't mope around at home. Now go and find something suitable to wear. I noticed you didn't make much effort for Almack's. I shall expect better of you today. Wear your best gown, the jonquil muslin.'

'That makes me look sallow, Mama, and…'

'Nonsense. Now do stop arguing with me. You're giving me a headache.'

With a heartfelt sigh Ianthe left the room, resigned to an evening of utter boredom. Unless… No, surely there was little hope of the Marquess attending a musical soiree. Or was there?

The occasion was as awful as she had feared. Their hostess had been too parsimonious to hire a professional musician or singer, and instead had called upon a number of young ladies of her acquaintance to show off their skills with the pianoforte, the harp or their voices, Serena among them. It was purgatory.

Ianthe cringed as yet another girl warbled her way through a ballad of some sort, missing several notes and mangling the rest. She decided that enough was enough. 'Mama, I'm going outside for a moment, I feel faint,' she whispered to her mother, fanning herself vigorously to demonstrate just how ill she felt. Lady Templeton frowned impatiently, but nodded her acquiescence.

'Very well, but don't be long.'

As she had had the forethought to sit at the end of a row, Ianthe was able to slip out fairly easily, and when the footman closed the door behind her, mercifully shutting off the screeching, she breathed a sigh of relief.

'That bad, is it?' The voice, oozing lazy amusement, came from just to her right, and Ianthe jumped. Turning quickly, she found the Marquess of Wyckeham smiling at her before giving her a conspiratorial wink. She couldn't help but smile back at him.

'Yes, absolutely excruciating. It was making me feel quite faint, so I thought I'd come out for some fresh air.'

'Very wise of you, I must say.'

'And what would be your excuse for skulking out here, my lord?' she dared to tease him.

'I arrived late, so naturally I couldn't be so rude as to interrupt. Far better to wait out here until it's over, don't you think?' His eyes were sparkling with amusement and she decided she liked the way they crinkled at the corners. It was most attractive.

'Definitely, and it has the added bonus of allowing you to retain both your sanity and your hearing,' she said.

He laughed and held out his arm. 'May I escort you onto the terrace? Or would you prefer to sit down somewhere?'

'The terrace would be lovely, thank you.'

She placed her hand on the proffered arm. His coat sleeve felt slightly rough under her fingers, but she could also feel the warmth of his skin radiating through the material and the hard muscle underneath. The sensation sent a shimmer of excitement through her.

He led her outside through a large French window and over to the balustrade of the terrace, where they stood in the semi-darkness, breathing in deep lungfuls of delicious night air. Lanterns had been hung in the nearby trees and they twinkled prettily when the wind stirred the branches, making the garden look almost ethereal.

Ianthe was aware of the fact that she ought not to be out here on her own with the Marquess, but she had been unable to resist. She found him fascinating, but she also knew he had a reputation with the ladies, while she was young and naïve and perhaps easy prey. As if reading her thoughts, he said reassuringly, 'Don't worry, you are quite safe with me. I only seduce innocent young ladies on Wednesdays.'

'Today is Wednesday.'

'Is it? Good Lord, I must mean Thursdays, then.'

She laughed and shook her head in mock exasperation. 'You're impossible.'

'So I've been told. I have to live up to my nickname, you know.'

'You know about that?'

'Of course.' He smiled ruefully. 'The gossips aren't exactly subtle.'

'Yes, well, you're also very generous – I must thank you for the flowers you sent this morning. They were exquisite.'

'You need not thank me unless you wish to,' he said teasingly.

'Of course I wish to, I only meant... Oh, you know exactly what I meant.'

He chuckled. 'Sorry, couldn't resist. You are lovely when you're flustered, but you don't need to be when you're in my company, you know. I don't bite and contrary to popular belief, I do have a sense of humour.'

His strange compliment made her tingle

with pleasure, but she tried to continue with the flippant tone as she didn't want him to notice. 'I'm very glad to hear it. I can't stand people who don't.'

'You are also very forthright. I like that.'

'Do you? Not many men find that a desirable trait in a woman.'

'Well, they should. Can't abide mealy-mouthed females, they are so dull. No, give me a spirited one any day.'

They were standing very close, their forearms touching where they rested on the balustrade, and Ianthe was suddenly very aware of him staring at her intently. She wondered whether he felt it too, this strange connection between them, then told herself not to be so silly. He was a man of the world; merely standing close to a young girl surely wouldn't affect him one whit. Especially one who was not a diamond of the first water like her sister. She looked away, feeling her face suffuse with colour.

'I … perhaps we ought to return indoors,' she said. 'The concert must surely be nearly over by now.'

'Yes, and no doubt there will be a stampede as everyone tries to escape as quickly as possible, in case the young ladies are contemplating an encore.'

She laughed at the image his words conjured up. 'Then hadn't we better position ourselves so that we are first in the queue for supper?'

'Good idea.' He held out his arm once more, and brought her inside and over to the double doors leading into an adjoining room that had been set aside for eating. The two footmen flanking the entrance opened the doors just as they arrived, and at the same time people began to spill out of the other room. 'Just in time,' Wyckeham remarked and was about to lead her over to a table when an elderly matron hailed him loudly.

'Wyckeham, my boy, haven't seen you for ages. Heard you were in town, wife-hunting on your nephew's behalf. That true? Come and talk to me.'

He turned to shrug apologetically at Ianthe. 'I'm sorry, but that is my great-aunt Augusta. Would you excuse me? Perhaps I shall see you later.'

'Of course. Thank you for keeping me company.'

'It was a pleasure I would not have missed for the world.'

She watched him walk away and gave herself a stern talking-to. *He is not for you, and he is not paying you any more attention than he would any other young lady. You heard the woman; he's helping his nephew select a suitable wife and he's merely passing the time by flirting a little. Don't read anything into it.*

But she couldn't help but wish it were otherwise.

Jason listened to his great-aunt's monologue with only one ear, while surreptitiously keeping an eye on Ianthe across the room. He saw her glancing in his direction several times, and then averting her gaze when she caught him watching her. She looked positively glowing and if anyone had asked him, he would have stated unequivocally that she was by far the prettier of the twins.

He had left Almack's the previous evening, determined to ignore the attraction he had felt for her, but somehow he had found it impossible to stay away from the soiree, once Robert informed him the sisters would be there. He wanted to see her again, talk to her some more, listen to her enchanting laughter, and he hadn't been disappointed. Out on the terrace just now, she had sparkled, her ready wit and obvious intelligence pleasing him as much as her lovely countenance. He realised he simply enjoyed being with her.

'Oh, this is ridiculous,' he muttered.

'What was that?' Great-aunt Augusta frowned at him.

'Nothing, dear aunt, nothing. I was just looking at that young fop's waistcoat over there. Ridiculous.' He nodded towards a young man sporting a particularly garish garment in a violent shade of lime green.

'Sorry to have interrupted you, do go on.'

His aunt rambled on and Jason's thoughts returned to his previous preoccupation. What was the matter with him? A spurt of irritation shot through him and he frowned at no one in particular. Surely he hadn't fallen for Miss Templeton? She was too young, too inexperienced, too … altogether perfect. He hadn't come to London to find a bride for himself and he didn't want to fall in love, but did one have a choice in these matters? It simply happened.

He sighed and closed his eyes for a moment, then interrupted his great-aunt in mid-flow. 'Excuse me, Aunt Augusta, but I see an acquaintance over there is trying to attract my attention. Fellow's been after a word with me for ages, so I'd better oblige. Wonderful to see you looking so well, I'll speak with you soon.'

And before she could protest, he'd left her side and headed across the room. Not to speak to anyone though, but to leave. He had to get out of here so he could be alone with his thoughts.

He had a decision to make.

The following morning further floral tributes arrived, but this time Ianthe only received one. It was enough, however, since it was a huge bouquet of yellow roses with a card signed simply 'W'. Her heart began to beat a little faster.

Serena, who had had no fewer than four posies this time, frowned across the table at her sister. 'Who is that from? That silly fool who pretends he's a poet? I saw him hanging on your every word last night.'

'No, it's not from Sir Roland. I believe it's from Wyckeham.' Ianthe tried to say this in an offhand manner, as if she didn't care one iota who had sent the flowers, but Serena shot out of her chair nonetheless and came to look at the card before fixing her sister with a suspicious glare.

'He didn't send *me* flowers today. What does he mean by it? He barely spoke to us last night.'

Ianthe shrugged. 'I have no idea. Perhaps it's his idea of a joke?'

'Well, I don't find it amusing in the slightest. I shall have words with him tonight at Lady Betterley's ball.'

'Serena!' Lady Templeton looked scandalised. 'You cannot possibly chastise a man you barely know for not sending you flowers. Honestly, have you no sense?'

'I didn't mean it quite like that, Mama. I only meant, I shall make sure I have a chance to speak to him, to make certain he knows I'm the one who is interested in marriage, not Ianthe.'

Ianthe frowned. 'And why shouldn't I be interested in marriage? You keep saying that, as if I'm some sort of nun. I'd rather not spend the rest of my life alone, thank you very much.'

'Well, you'd better be nice to your poet then,' Serena laughed. 'If you can stomach a life of having bad verse quoted at you.'

'Perhaps someone more suitable will offer for me.'

'Don't be ridiculous. Why would anyone be interested in *you?*' Serena swept a disdainful glance over Ianthe's ill-fitting gown. 'Besides, you said you'd be happy with a country squire. You'd do better to go home and attend the local assembly balls.' She headed for the door. 'Come, Mama, we must go shopping. I need a new pair of gloves as I, for one, don't want to look like a dowd.'

'But I only just bought you some, Serena, and your Papa said that we're not to spend any more money now.'

'Mama! I need a pair to match my new ballgown. Surely you don't expect me to look a fright? How will I catch a husband then?'

'Oh, well, no, I suppose...' As always, Lady Templeton gave in and Ianthe shook her head after them, wondering why Serena always had her way. It simply wasn't fair.

Serena's barb had struck home, and Ianthe decided to pay more attention to the way she dressed for the evening's ball. She didn't have any really fashionable gowns like her sister – once it became clear that no one was interested in courting her, Lady Templeton had decreed that their meagre funds had to be used exclusively for Serena's wardrobe, and Ianthe was forced to wear the dresses she'd worn in the country, which were now sadly outdated. She hadn't minded until now.

Well, perhaps I can at least refurbish one of my own gowns, she thought and went in search of her mother's French maid, who was quick with a needle and who had a soft spot for Ianthe because of the latter's proficiency in French.

'Dupont, I'd be very grateful if you could take a look through my wardrobe and see if there is anything worth wearing in there. I'm tired of looking like a provincial nobody.'

'Mais bien sur, Mademoiselle, I will 'elp you. Allons-y.'

Together, they went through every gown Ianthe owned and managed to find one that was reasonably well cut and might look less provincial with a few alterations. 'Regardez, this one will look elegante if I take off all the trimmings.' Dupont held up a pale green silk gown that shimmered in the light, but which was at present covered with lace, bows and all sorts of other embellishments that had put Ianthe off wearing it.

'Yes, you're right. I should never have allowed Mama to tell the dressmaker to add all that rubbish. Please, go ahead and do whatever you want with it.'

When Dupont brought the gown back some time later and Ianthe tried it on, she was thrilled. 'Oh, thank you, you've improved it no end. Merci beaucoup. What a treasure you are.'

'De rien.' Dupont beamed at her and winked. 'I 'ope you steal some of the other Mademoiselle's young men.'

Ianthe smiled back. Just one of them would do nicely.

Lady Betterley's ballroom was so crowded,

Ianthe thought to herself that no one would be able to dance. Nonetheless, to her amazement her dance card soon filled up, although she kept a few dances free just in case she needed a breathing space, or so she told herself.

'Ladies, have you saved us any dances?' The voice, deep, melodious and strangely unsettling, startled Ianthe out of her contemplation of the throng and she turned to find Lord Wyckeham and his nephew bowing to Serena and Lady Templeton.

'But of course, we've only just arrived so there are plenty left,' Serena lied and was quick to thrust her card at the Marquess before Ianthe had time to so much as greet him.

Wyckeham scrawled his name somewhere seemingly at random, which made Serena frown slightly, then handed the card to his nephew before holding out his hand for Ianthe's. His eyes seemed to rake over her as he took in the green dress and he nodded in approval. 'Lovely,' he murmured, so quietly that only she heard him. Ianthe felt her cheeks heat up and realized that it was his opinion she had sought. No one else's mattered. She was glad now that she had made an effort with her appearance.

When he gave her card back, she glanced at it and noticed that he had claimed the supper dance. She blinked and looked up, opening her mouth to ask if he really wished for that particular one, but shut it again when he winked at her, a mischievous glint in his eyes. 'I shall see you later,' he said before disappearing through the crowd.

Serena frowned after him and looked at her own card. 'He's only claimed one dance,' she complained.

'All the more for me,' Mr Warwycke smiled, and Serena had to be content with that.

By the time the supper dance was announced, Ianthe was more than ready for a break. Her feet were throbbing from so much unaccustomed exercise and her stomach ached with hunger. As Wyckeham came to claim her, however, she forgot any discomfort and followed him onto the floor. It was another waltz, and just as at Almack's, he twirled her round the room gracefully.

'Are you enjoying the evening?' he asked.

'Yes, thanks to you,' she replied, then felt herself blush as she realised that the words had come out all wrong. 'I meant to say that, because you danced with me at Almack's, everyone else has decided to follow suit, so I am no longer a wallflower.'

He smiled a lazy smile that sent waves of heat through her body. 'And there was I, thinking you meant that you were enjoying only this particular dance with me,' he teased.

'Of course I am, but...'

'But you're too well brought-up to ever say such a thing. Unlike your sister, who I believe would use any means to further her ends.'

'Oh dear, what did she say to you?' Ianthe felt both shame and pleasure that the

Marquess seemed to see through Serena so easily. She ought to be mostly embarrassed, but she was happy to find at least one man who didn't immediately fall for Serena's wiles.

'Nothing I am unable to handle,' he said enigmatically.

When the dance came to an end, he held out his arm and escorted her towards the supper room. They had only taken a few steps, however, when Serena's voice hailed them from behind.

'There you are. Mr Warwycke and I thought we should find a table for four. So much more fun than sitting alone, don't you think?'

Wyckeham stopped to let them catch up, and Ianthe thought she saw a look of impatience dart across his countenance, but he said nothing. The others were behind them in a trice, and Ianthe turned to walk with the Marquess into the supper room. Before she had moved more than a foot, however, she was yanked backwards and there was a loud tearing noise behind her. She threw a look over her shoulder and gasped.

'Oh, no, my dress!' Searching with her fingers behind her back, she found that the lovely green silk had been torn where the skirt joined the bodice, and the jagged edges of material flapped open, revealing a hole so large she must be showing the world a goodly portion of her shift.

'I am so sorry, I must have stepped on the hem,' Serena said, her eyes sparkling with victory. 'You'll have to go and mend it as best you can.' She turned to Wyckeham and placed her hand on his arm, where only a minute before Ianthe's had rested. 'We can wait for her at the table, else we'll starve to death. Come, gentlemen, let us eat.'

Wyckeham scowled at Serena, but she had already turned to urge Mr Warwycke to join them and didn't notice.

'Would you like me to escort you to the ladies' withdrawing room?' he asked Ianthe, but she shook her head, too angry and mortified to speak. She had known Serena was capable of great malice, but this was the outside of enough.

'I'll be fine,' she managed to grit out at last. 'Please, go ahead without me, I'll catch up.'

But as she turned to make her way to the ladies' room, she knew that the sort of repairs needed to her dress would take ages, by which time supper would be over and Serena would have charmed the Marquess completely, the way she did all other men. Despite the fact that he had seen through her earlier, he was probably just like everyone else and would fall prey to Serena's beauty in the end. It was inevitable.

Ianthe took a deep breath and straightened her spine. Well, if he was that fickle, he wasn't worth having.

CHAPTER THREE

Ianthe was the only person in the breakfast room the next day, which suited her perfectly. She didn't think she could find it in herself to be civil to her sister after what she had done the previous evening, and their mother was just as bad. She had insisted that it was merely an unfortunate accident.

'In such a crush, it could happen any time,' Lady Templeton had said soothingly, as always anxious to avoid a confrontation. 'You were just unlucky.'

'Accident, hah,' Ianthe muttered to herself now. 'Not likely with Serena at daggers drawn.'

A knock on the door heralded Balfour, who held out a silver salver with a card on it. 'There's a gentleman in the hall who claims that you are going riding with him this morning. Had you forgotten, Miss?'

Balfour would be well aware she had made no such arrangements, else she would have told him, but he was too well-trained to bat an eyelid.

'I…' She glanced at the card, which had 'Wyckeham' printed in large letters, and her heart flipped over. 'Yes, oh dear, how silly of me. Would you be so kind as to ask him to wait? I'll have to change, but I won't keep him long.'

'Of course, Miss.'

'Thank you. And Balfour, could you have my horse saddled, please?'

'No need, Miss, the gentleman has brought a mount for you. No doubt you had forgotten that as well.' Ianthe thought she saw a small smile curve the butler's mouth as he left the room, and she suddenly had the feeling that they were co-conspirators somehow.

She rushed upstairs and changed into her riding habit which, if not precisely fashion-able, was at least a becoming shade of cornflower blue that she knew accentuated the colour of her eyes. It was done in the military style, which suited her figure, and as she came downstairs to find his lordship pacing the hall, it made her feel better to know that she looked as well as she could.

The look in his eyes as he caught sight of her confirmed this and made her smile. 'I trust I haven't kept you waiting for too long, my lord?' she said while he bowed over her hand. 'You should have reminded me of our, er, proposed outing yesterday.'

He tried to look contrite, but failed signally as Ianthe noticed the sparkle of mischief in his eyes yet again. 'Yes, indeed I should have, but I wasn't sure you'd accept the invitation. Sometimes not giving people time to think about something makes them act on the spur of the moment. I was counting on that.'

'I see.' Ianthe could have told him that she would have jumped at the chance to go riding with him any time, but thought it best not to in case it made her seem too eager for his company.

'And you didn't keep me waiting,' he added. 'In fact, you were remarkably quick, but then I knew you would be.'

'How could you possibly know that?'

He grinned at her. 'Because I could tell from the very first time I set eyes on you that you're not like other women.'

Ianthe blinked at the compliment – if compliment it was – but he didn't allow her time to think about it. Instead, he led her outside and helped her onto the back of quite the most magnificent horse she had ever seen, a glossy black thoroughbred with long mane and tail, brushed to perfection. 'I made enquiries,' Wyckeham said, 'and was told you're a bruising rider. I hope he'll suit you?'

Ianthe beamed. 'He's perfect. I can't wait to put him through his paces.'

'Let's go, then.'

They set off for the park, a groom riding slightly behind them for the sake of propriety, and Ianthe was not disappointed. As it was early, and few people were about, they flouted the unwritten rules and let the horses have a good gallop. Ianthe enjoyed herself immensely, and was pleased when the horse followed her every lead. As they slowed to a walk, she bent over his neck to pat him and saw his ears twitching when she told him he was a gorgeous boy. She smiled at Wyckeham again. 'I think he likes me. What's his name?'

'Midnight. I thought he'd be perfect for you, he's the colour of your hair.'

They were now riding side by side along Rotten Row on the south side of Hyde Park and there were still only a few other riders about. Ianthe didn't care since she found the usual crowd there a bore. Without thinking, she said so.

Wyckeham laughed. 'Indeed, one can almost imagine that one is in the country today. But don't you prefer town living? Most young ladies do.'

'No, not at all. I can't wait to go home, in fact. All this forced merriment is very taxing and I find everyone false and back-stabbing.

In the country, people may gossip, but it's never seemed to me to be as malicious as it is here.'

'You don't like balls and routs?' His eyes searched hers as if he wanted to make sure.

'No, it's all so superficial. Forced gaiety. I feel I'm merely on show, a performer in some strange play. Country assemblies are much more fun.'

'So you wouldn't mind living most of the year in the country then?'

'Not at all. I would love it.'

'And would you like to live in the country with me?'

Ianthe gasped in surprise and stared at him, before turning away in confusion. She felt her cheeks flaming with both shock and embarrassment. Was he asking her to become his mistress? After only three days' acquaintance! Anger stirred inside her. What did he take her for? She may not be the toast of the town, but she wasn't that desperate. 'Really, my lord, I don't think...'

'Wyckeham! Hadn't thought to see you

out of bed so early.'

This greeting, drawled in a rather exaggerated way, cut Ianthe's sentence off and she looked round to find Wyckeham scowling at a man who resembled him slightly, although he was somewhat smaller in build, his features more finely chiselled. Seated next to the man on his own horse was young Mr Warwycke, or Robert as he had asked them to call him last night, looking decidedly worse for wear. His eyes were almost crossing in an attempt to focus on them and his clothes were in complete disarray. A distinct aroma of alcohol emanated from him and Ianthe unconsciously wrinkled her nose.

'Gervaise,' the Marquess replied curtly to the stranger and then nodded at his dishevelled nephew. 'So that's where you got to last night, Rob. I wondered.'

Robert had the grace to look sheepish and couldn't quite meet his uncle's eye, but Wyckeham didn't look at him for long. Instead he returned his gaze to the other man, who shrugged and pulled out a snuff box, from which he helped himself to a large pinch.

'A night on the town, you know how it is. I was delighted to show our young kinsman the best places to find entertainment.' The man smiled, but the smile didn't quite reach his eyes, which appeared to Ianthe to be dark and cold, fathomless in fact. She shivered involuntarily.

'Yes, I'm sure you were,' Wyckeham replied, his mouth an uncompromising line of disapproval now. 'So how many gaming halls did you manage to visit?'

'Only about four, I believe,' Gervaise replied airily, then threw a speculative glance at Ianthe. 'But this isn't a subject fit for a lady's ears. Aren't you going to introduce us, coz?'

Wyckeham looked as if he wished to avoid this at all cost, but good manners dictated that he must. 'Miss Templeton, this is a distant relative of mine, Gervaise Warwycke. Gervaise, Miss Ianthe Templeton.'

'Ah, one of the famous twins one has

heard so much about.' Gervaise stood up in the saddle and gave her an exaggerated bow, while running his eyes over her from top to toe and back again in a manner that made her skin crawl.

'How do you do?' she said, unwilling to engage in conversation with him.

Wyckeham, glancing at her, said, 'We'd better be on our way. Gentlemen.' He nodded curtly at both of them, and threw a parting shot over his shoulder at Robert. 'Get yourself home and into the bath. Then ask Cook for a tisane. You're going to need it.'

A dark shadow seemed to have descended upon them and they rode back to the Templeton house in silence. Ianthe decided that now was not the time to discuss Wyckeham's strange proposal, if that was what it had been. Perhaps if she pretended it had never happened, he wouldn't refer to it again. To her consternation, however, as the Marquess helped her down from the horse, he held her close to him for a moment, much too close for comfort and certainly not within the limits of propriety.

She glanced up at him with a frown to remonstrate, but found that he was looking down at her, an intense expression in his eyes, and she forgot what she had been about to say.

'I didn't mean to offend you,' he said softly. 'We will return to our conversation some other time, when I will try to express myself more clearly. And I'm sorry if I've been like a bear with a sore head, but I'm afraid meeting Gervaise always has that effect on me. Can't stand the fellow.'

Ianthe took a deep breath to steady herself. Being held by him was disrupting her thought processes and she wasn't sure what to make of his enigmatic words. She took refuge in common courtesy. 'Well, thank you for taking me riding, my lord. I enjoyed it immensely.'

His eyes seemed to bore into hers and she wondered for a wild moment if he was about to kiss her, but he obviously thought better of it. 'You're welcome. We should arrange another such outing soon. Will I see you again tonight?'

She nodded. 'If you're going to Mrs Etchilhampton's rout, then yes, no doubt our paths will cross.' She tried for a nonchalant tone, so as not to give the impression that she was eager for his company.

'I'll make sure of it,' he said, before finally letting her go. Ianthe felt almost bereft and turned quickly to mount the steps to the front door so that he wouldn't see what effect he was having on her, but before she reached it, he added gruffly, 'Save me the supper dance – and tell your sister that if she ruins your gown again, she'll rue the day she was born.'

CHAPTER FOUR

Ianthe was in a quandary. She had no more remotely attractive dresses to wear, and the green gown, which she had planned to use again, was beyond repair according to Dupont. Appealing to her mother for help would be no use, as Ianthe knew very well that there was no more money. Her father had allocated a certain sum for his daughters' coming-out – more than he could really afford, she knew – and they had exceeded this already, mostly because of Serena.

No, she would have to take matters into her own hands.

When Serena and Lady Templeton went out to pay a morning visit, Ianthe crept into Serena's room and opened the wardrobe which was bulging with garments. Ianthe quickly looked through them and found what she had been searching for, thrust into a corner. An ice-blue ball gown of shot silk embellished with huge pink fake roses round the hem and neckline that Serena had declared too frumpish for words.

'I'm sorry, Mama, but nothing in the world would persuade me to wear that. Send it back,' she had decreed.

Of course, Lady Templeton could do no such thing since the dress had been made to her exact specification and was already paid for. Instead, it had languished at the back of the wardrobe for several weeks, while Lady Templeton hoped Serena would change her mind. Ianthe pulled it out and returned to her room, calling for Dupont.

'Oui, Mademoiselle? Oh la la, what 'ave we 'ere? Quelle horreur!'

'Yes, isn't it awful? But I thought that if I remove the roses, it would be quite elegant. The only problem is that I'm taller than Serena, so it's not long enough. Could you help me find something to lengthen it with, please?'

73

'Mais oui, I will 'ave a look.'

Dupont unearthed an old gown with a wide silver lace trim around the hem. 'Look, this will be agreeable, non? I will cut it off.'

'Oh, yes, it's perfect. Do you think that if we work together, we can have it finished by this evening? Otherwise I can't go out. There is no way I am wearing my old gowns again. Not now that…'

She stopped herself from revealing the exact reason. There was no need for Dupont to know that. The little Frenchwoman smiled, however, as if she could guess. 'Don't worry, we can do it and you will look wonderful, je promesse.'

'I can't thank you enough.'

Dupont leaned closer and whispered, 'Just promise me that if you ever marry, please to take me with you when you leave. Your maman, she is nice lady, but very…'

'Demanding? Impossible?' Ianthe smiled. 'Of course – I wouldn't dream of leaving you behind.'

Ianthe purposely waited to go downstairs until the very last moment, when the others were already waiting in the hall and the carriage had been called for. Serena was talking to their mother, but broke off to frown at Ianthe as soon as she caught sight of her. 'Isn't that...? It is! Mama, she is wearing my gown, and ... what have you done to it? Go and take it off at once, I won't have you stealing my things.'

'I had nothing else to wear since you saw fit to ruin my only decent gown,' Ianthe said coolly. 'Besides, there's no time to change now, is there, Mama? We don't want to be late.'

'Indeed,' Lady Templeton agreed.

'But, Mama, she's stolen it – been in my room, and gone through my things. It's intolerable.'

'Enough, Serena, you have more gowns than you can possibly wish for. Surely you can spare your sister one? And moreover, one you refused to wear, if my memory serves me. Now let us be on our way and I want no more foolishness from either of you.'

Lady Templeton sounded unusually stern, so much so that even Serena did her bidding without further protest. Ianthe was astoished, but pleased, that her mother had taken her side for once, but judging by Serena's expression, she may come to regret her coup. Time enough to worry about that later, however.

Mrs Etchilhampton's rout was not quite as crowded as that lady would have liked, but it was nonetheless well attended and Ianthe couldn't immediately spot Wyckeham when they arrived. Quite why she wanted to see him again, she couldn't say. If he was going to humiliate her by offering her a carte blanche, she ought to stay out of his way, but somehow she thought she must have misunderstood. It was not the done thing to ask respectable young girls to be one's mistress, no matter how impecunious they might be, and although he had said he had to live up to his reputation as 'Lord Wicked', she was sure he had been joking. She felt strongly that the real Wyckeham was a true gentleman.

As she stood with her mother and sister, only half-listening to Serena's flirtations with all the young men who flocked to her side, she noticed the Marquess's relative, Gervaise, enter the room with Robert in tow. The two seemed on remarkably good terms and headed straight for the card room rather than towards the young ladies waiting for partners. Ianthe frowned. It seemed unlike Robert to be so rude.

'So you noticed it too, then?'

The smooth voice was barely audible behind Ianthe's right shoulder, and she realised Wyckeham wished for no one but her to hear him. His softly-spoken words sent a frisson of pleasure down her spine and she turned to see him scowling after Gervaise and Robert. He sighed and looked at her instead, his gaze immediately softening.

'I'm sorry, I shouldn't burden you with my problems,' he said. 'Did you save me a dance?'

She nodded. 'The one you asked for.'

'Good girl.' He scrawled a W on her card and handed it back. 'I'll speak to you later. For now, I've got my work cut out keeping Rob out of mischief.'

He was gone almost as quickly as he had appeared, and since Serena and their mother were still engrossed in conversation with the Earl and one of his friends, they hadn't even noticed Wyckeham's presence. Secretly, Ianthe was glad – as it meant he hadn't asked Serena for a dance too.

'So did you manage to find Robert?' Ianthe asked when she and Wyckeham sat down to eat their supper at a small table in a corner. It was hidden away behind a large pot plant, and Ianthe had a suspicion that the Marquess had bribed one of the footmen to keep it free especially for them. She wasn't complaining, however, since it kept them away from Serena.

Wyckeham sighed. 'Yes, but unfortunately he seems to consider Gervaise his new best friend and the fount of all knowledge. Nothing I say registers. I had warned him to be on his guard against older men who try to inveigle him into gaming and, er … suchlike, but because Gervaise is family of sorts, Rob thinks he's different and won't listen to me.'

'And is he? Different, I mean.'

Wyckeham regarded her with one raised eyebrow and a sardonic smile. 'What do you think?'

'I have to confess I took an instant dislike to him, but I don't know why.'

'Then you are more astute than my nephew.' Wyckeham shook his head. 'No, Gervaise is no saint, far from it. Sadly though, I will have to let Rob make a few mistakes on his own. It's the only way he'll learn. Let's not talk about that, though; we have more important matters to discuss.'

'We do?' Ianthe felt a small stirring of unease and butterflies danced in her stomach. She wasn't sure she was going to like what he had to say.

He smiled, which made the butterflies

redouble their efforts. She took a bite of her lobster pate to try and settle them, but found it hard to swallow.

'Are you still certain you're not afraid of me? I know you must have heard all the rumours by now.'

'No, I'm not afraid.' As she looked into his eyes, she knew this was the truth. She was absolutely certain he would never hurt her, although quite how she could be so sure, she had no idea.

'Excellent, because I can assure you none of it is true. Well, only the part about me hating my wife. Elizabeth was a spoiled termagant and I was happy to be rid of her.'

'I ... should you be telling me this?' Ianthe didn't feel it was the done thing to talk about one's dead wife in such terms.

'Yes. I feel that nothing but the truth will do between us. I know you are as straightforward as I am, so I won't insult your intelligence by pretending something that isn't true.'

Ianthe nodded. She appreciated him not

underestimating her understanding. 'Why, then, did you marry her?' she asked, curiosity overtaking her scruples.

'I was young and stupid, she was beautiful and an expert at deceit...' He shrugged. 'I never saw her true colours until it was much too late and, just like Robert, I refused to listen to wiser counsel. It's a common story.'

'Yes, so I've heard.' She couldn't help glancing over to where Serena was seated with Lord Somerville and Wyckeham chuckled.

'You're thinking that poor Somerville is going to end up like that, aren't you? Do you think we ought to rescue him?'

'No, no, Serena's not all bad. I'm sure that once she is married, she will make her chosen husband very happy. She's just enjoying being the centre of attention at the moment.'

'Hmm, well, you know her best, I suppose.'

'Either way, it's none of our business, is it?'

He smiled again. 'You're right. I think he'll have to learn the hard way, poor man. But never mind that, let us return to our previous subject of discussion.'

'Oh, yes, well...' Ianthe felt the butterflies return with a vengeance.

'What I was trying to ask you in the park before that fool Gervaise interrupted me,' he continued, 'was, if you were married to someone, would you mind spending most of the year in the country with him rather than in London?'

'M-married?' Ianthe felt relief flooding her. If he was only speaking rhetorically and mentioning marriage, he couldn't be thinking of any other arrangements. 'Oh, in that case I wouldn't mind at all. I told you, I'm not enjoying town life much.'

'Excellent. I'm only asking because that's the way I see it, too, and it's not something I'm prepared to compromise on. I despise London society.'

Ianthe waited for him to continue, her breath coming in shallow gasps. Was he saying what she thought he was?

He made sure no one was looking their

way, then leaned forward and took one of her hands in his. 'So if I were to ask your father for your hand in marriage, you wouldn't refuse me on the grounds that you'd miss out on the social whirl?'

'N-no, certainly not,' she managed to stammer out. 'But you barely know me. I mean, how can you be certain that we'll suit? We only met a few days ago.' There were a dozen other questions whirling round her mind that she wanted to ask him, but dare not. Why her, and not Serena? Was he really serious? Did he love her? She shook her head slightly in an attempt to clear it. It was all too much to take in.

'I know enough to realise that we would suit very well, but I know that you are very young and if you'd rather that I waited a while and courted you properly, I will do so. Only, I feel the same way you do about these infernal balls and parties, and I'd rather not stay in London a moment longer than I must. I shall if you wish me to, though, of course.'

'No! No, please, go ahead and ... er, speak to my father. I mean, if you're sure that's what you would like.'

'Is it what you wish?'

She looked into his eyes and saw a flash of desire that should have frightened her but, strangely, didn't. 'Yes. Yes, it is.' He may not have declared undying love for her, but the prospect of spending the rest of her life with him, on whatever terms, was an opportunity she simply couldn't pass by. She knew she would never want to marry anyone else, now that she had met him.

He held her gaze for another heartbeat before letting go of her hand. 'Good, that's settled then,' he said. 'I'll be away for a few days, but as soon as I return I'll come and see you and we can make plans.'

She couldn't trust herself to speak, so she simply nodded acquiescence and prayed that her father would give his consent.

CHAPTER FIVE

Serena smiled. 'It would seem the Marquess has found better things to do with his time than dance attendance on my sister. He's been gone for nearly a week now.' She batted her eyelashes at Gervaise Warwycke, who appeared to be as susceptible to her charms as every other man under the sun apart from Wyckeham. She was hoping Gervaise would be able to help her find a way to ensnare the Marquess, but of course she couldn't say so outright.

'Do you think so?' he drawled. 'I wouldn't count on it. He plays his cards close to his chest and you never know what he's going to do next.'

Slightly alarmed, Serena fanned herself rapidly with the delicate ostrich fan she had accepted from the Earl of Somerville in secret, even though young ladies were not supposed to receive gifts except from their betrothed. She wanted Somerville to think that she was going to marry him – and she might, if her other plans didn't work out – so she had accepted the present with a few murmured promises, but in truth, for the moment, she was merely stringing him along.

'You think Wyckeham is interested in Ianthe?' Serena had looked on with mounting fury at Mrs Etchilhampton's rout as the Marquess ignored her and led her sister in to supper, then left without so much as dancing with Serena. It was not to be borne.

'Who's to say? But if I were you, I'd make sure he couldn't be, just to be on the safe side, don't you know?'

Serena tried to read Gervaise's expression, but he was his usual urbane self, giving nothing away. She recognised a fellow conspirator, however, and he had that look about him as of someone who was plotting something. It sent a thrill down her spine. 'Now how do

you suggest I do that?' she purred, her eyebrows raised flirtatiously. 'I can't very well
send her packing back to the country
without an excuse.'

'No, indeed, but there are ways of forcing
a girl to rusticate.'

'None that I can think of, but I'd wager
you have an idea or two, am I right?' She
tapped him playfully on the arm with her
fan and he nodded, a small smile playing
about his mouth. It was not a nice smile and
it almost made Serena shudder, but then
she remembered that they were talking
about Ianthe.

'I would suggest an outing to Richmond
Park – yourself, young Robert, me and your
sister, plus two others. We can travel in a
carriage for four and my phaeton. You come
with me on the drive to the park, then you
make sure your sister is my companion on
the way home. Leave the rest to me.'

'And why would you help me in this way?'
Serena asked, a trifle suspicious as to his
motives. If he thought she would waste her

charms on someone as low-ranking as him, he was mistaken.

'Let's just say that it is in my interests for the Marquess to stay a bachelor. After Robert, I'm next in line to inherit the marquessate and who knows, accidents may happen. The boy is young and wild.'

Serena was slightly taken aback by his callous words, but decided not to read too much into them. He was right, after all; accidents and illnesses often interfered in lines of inheritance and if he wanted to make sure the odds were in his favour, then who could blame him? The thought of Ianthe brought low was much more interesting and she tried not to let her mounting excitement show. She wanted to ask him what he was planning, but decided she had better not. If she didn't know, she could never be accused of having had a hand in her sister's downfall. For downfall it certainly would be, judging by the look in Gervaise's eye. She nodded.

'Very well. Would Wednesday suit? I'll ask two friends and Ianthe, and you bring

Robert. Say at midday?'

'Agreed. Just pray that Wyckeham doesn't return before then.'

A week and a half had gone by and there was no sign of Wyckeham. Ianthe had begun to think that perhaps she had dreamed their entire conversation or, if she hadn't, he had thought better of such a crazy idea and changed his mind. Why would he want to marry her anyway? She had no dowry and not a great deal else to recommend her either.

When Serena suggested that she come along on an outing to Richmond Park, she decided she may as well. She had nothing else to do and if she stayed at home, she would only dwell on the Marquess's continued absence. As she came out of the house on the Wednesday and saw who their companions were, however, she almost had second thoughts, but the two Misses Gardiner were present as well, and this reassured her somewhat. There was safety in numbers.

'Is it not a lovely day, Ianthe?' Anne Gardiner enthused as Ianthe stepped into the carriage, helped by Robert who was an interesting shade of grey.

'Indeed. The sun is very bright, though, perhaps a trifle too much so for Mr Warwycke here?' Ianthe couldn't resist teasing the young man. It was very obvious that he had had a late night and was suffering the consequences.

He tried to smile, although it looked more like a grimace. 'No doubt some fresh air will do me good. All these ballrooms and … other establishments are so stuffy, you know.'

He didn't add much to the conversation on the way, however, but sat and stared fixedly at the road through the window, as if willing his breakfast to stay down. Ianthe almost felt sorry for him, but remembered Wyckeham's words – the young man had to learn things the hard way.

They had a pleasant enough afternoon; Gervaise could be entertaining when he set himself out to be. He regaled them with stories of his travels and mishaps on the Continent and the Misses Gardiner never stopped giggling. Even Robert perked up after some lunch and a few glasses of champagne and Ianthe found that she didn't have time to dwell on any distracting thoughts.

'Are you enjoying yourself, Miss Templeton?' Gervaise had come up behind Ianthe as she stood by the edge of a pond, throwing leftover pieces of bread to some appreciative ducks.

'Indeed, sir, it's nice to be away from the hustle and bustle of London.'

'I take it then that you are not a social butterfly like your sister?'

Ianthe shook her head. 'No, I'm afraid we have little in common, as is probably obvious to most people.'

'Oh, I don't know: you are both beautiful young ladies, albeit slightly different. One cannot help one's disposition and if you prefer the company of books, then I'm sure that is not a crime. A lady as lovely as yourself should surely be allowed to spend her time doing whatever she wishes.'

Ianthe felt decidedly uncomfortable with his fulsome compliments and was unsure how to answer. In the end, she merely said, 'Thank you, but I fear that not everyone thinks that way.'

They were interrupted by Serena, who as usual couldn't bear to be excluded from any conversation, and Ianthe was happy to go back to the others. There was something about Gervaise Warwycke that made her uneasy, and she wished now that she hadn't come.

'I suppose we had better set out for home,' Serena sighed. 'We ladies will need time to make ourselves beautiful for tonight's ball.' Ianthe saw her glance flirtatiously at both Robert and Gervaise, but Gervaise was the first to reply to this unsubtle fishing for a compliment.

'Surely that won't take you more than a few moments, Miss Templeton,' he said. 'Nature cannot be improved upon, you know.'

Ianthe turned her head away in disgust.

On their way back to the carriages, Serena suddenly stumbled and fell with a little shriek of pain. Gervaise and Robert rushed to her side, as did the Misses Gardiner, before Ianthe had a chance to reach her.

'Oh, my ankle! There was a rabbit hole, I didn't see it,' wailed Serena. 'Stupid animals, must they be forever digging? Ah, no, don't touch it!' She batted away Robert's questing hands.

'Please, Miss Templeton, let me have a look. I have some experience of these things,' Gervaise said calmly.

Serena nodded. 'Oh, very well, if you must.' Her bottom lip wobbled slightly and a tear trickled out of the corner of one eye. He felt her ankle under her skirts, obviously trying to probe as gently as he could, but she still winced.

'Hmm, yes, it's swollen, but nothing broken, I think. Probably just sprained. Allow me to carry you to the brougham. You mustn't put any weight on it.'

'If you say so.' Serena held up her arms and he lifted her, staggering slightly under her weight, but refusing Robert's offer of help.

It wasn't until Serena was ensconced in the carriage with Robert and the Misses Gardiner that Ianthe realised what that meant and began to smell a rat. 'You must ride back with Mr Warwycke in his phaeton, Ianthe. I need my friends here with me, and dear Robert will of course be a tower of strength.' Serena was playing the wounded martyr to the hilt, but Ianthe recognised it now for what it was – play-acting.

'I really don't think...' she began, but Serena cut her off.

'For heaven's sake, Ianthe, we will be right behind you, as you were on the way here. There will be no impropriety. Please, I just want to go home.' She managed to squeeze out a few more convincing tears and after sending her sister a narrowed glance, Ianthe gave up.

'Oh, very well.'

She allowed Gervaise to help her up onto the high seat of the phaeton, but tried to put as much distance between them as she could. He sent her an amused glance.

'I don't bite, you know, and I'm accounted quite a good whip.'

'I'm glad to hear it,' Ianthe replied, then stared straight ahead while he set the horses in motion.

They rode in silence for a while and Ianthe glanced back towards the brougham from time to time, to make sure it was keeping up with them. It was a slower conveyance, however, and with four passengers it wasn't able to travel as fast as the phaeton, which began to draw ahead. After they rounded a sharp bend, Gervaise suddenly whipped his team into a gallop and they set off at a cracking pace. His tiger, the diminutive groom who perched on the back of the phaeton and usually jumped down to hold the horses' heads whenever they stopped, had to hang on for dear life.

'No, stop! What are you doing?' Ianthe

cried out in panic, but he merely threw her a triumphant smile and urged on the horses to run even faster.

'One should always travel quickly in a carriage such as this,' he shouted, but she could barely hear him over the din of the horses' hooves and the whooshing noise of the wind. She had to hold on to the side with both hands so that the swaying motion didn't throw her out altogether.

Gervaise kept up this crazy pace for quite some time, until Ianthe thought the poor horses were going to expire, but then he suddenly turned sharply onto a smaller road, and soon a dilapidated inn came into view. There was no sign of the brougham, but then Ianthe hadn't expected there to be. As they came to a halt outside the inn, Ianthe felt her stomach muscles clench in fear. There was no doubt that Gervaise was up to something, and she was sure that whatever it was, he meant her ill.

She swore to herself that if she ever set eyes on her sister again, she would make her pay for this.

'Come down from the carriage, Miss Ianthe. We are going to have some refreshment before we continue our journey.'

Ianthe gazed down at Gervaise's outstretched hand and shook her head. 'No, thank you. I'd rather stay where I am.'

'It wasn't a request,' he said, his tone menacing now. 'Either you jump down by yourself or I'll pull you. And I won't be gentle, I can promise you that.'

Ianthe glared at him, but realised she had no choice. He wasn't as big as the Marquess by any means, but he was certainly stronger than her and she had no doubt he'd carry out his threat without any hesitation. A quick glance around showed her that there was no one in the vicinity on whom she could call for help, and so she had perforce to do his bidding. She gritted her teeth and jumped.

Before she had time to remonstrate, he grabbed her hand in an iron grip and dragged her into the taproom of the inn. Ianthe recoiled at the musty smell inside, a combination of tobacco smoke, stale ale, food, and overwhelming body odour. Half a dozen men were lounging about, but no one paid much attention to them apart from the landlord, who came sidling up looking anxious to please.

'A private parlour and be quick about it,' Gervaise ordered.

'Of course, sir, straight away. If you would follow me, please?'

The slovenly man led them down a narrow corridor and into a tiny room at the back of the inn, which was shabbily furnished and smelled as if the window hadn't been opened for years. Ianthe almost gagged and tried to turn in the doorway, but Geravise didn't let go of her arm and pulled her through with a vicious tug at her wrist.

'Bring victuals, please, landlord, and ale for myself and wine for the lady.'

'I don't want...' Ianthe began, but Gervaise turned on her and the words died in her throat. There was such menace in his eyes, she physically recoiled from him and stumbled backwards. The backs of her legs collided with a chair and she sat down abruptly.

'That's better,' Gervaise muttered and slammed the door shut after the obsequious man.

'What do you want with me?' Ianthe whispered, although she feared she knew only too well. She couldn't believe that her own sister had colluded with such a man to engineer her downfall.

'You'll find out in due course. We'll be staying here until it's dark, but for now all you have to do is sit here quietly and not make a fuss, is that understood? If I hear so much as a tiny protest out of you or a cry for help, you'll be very sorry.'

Ianthe nodded. She understood exactly what he was saying and for the moment, it behoved her to follow his orders. Meanwhile, she must try to find a way to escape. She simply couldn't let this happen to her, not now that there was so much at stake.

'I'm going to the tap room for a while. You're to stay in this room and not budge so much as an inch,' Gervaise told her after they had partaken of the tasteless meat pie and soggy vegetables brought by the landlord. Gervaise had grumbled about the fare, but ate heartily nonetheless, whereas Ianthe had only picked at it and left most of her portion on the plate.

She didn't reply, since she had every intention of trying to escape the minute he left the room, but he didn't seem to notice. She soon found out why he had so carelessly left her on her own – when she opened the door a crack, she came face to face with Gervaise's tiger, a small youth who nevertheless looked strong enough to catch her should she try to dart past. He grinned at her in a leering way that didn't bode well.

'Goin' somewhere, are ye?' he asked, and chuckled when Ianthe retreated back into the shabby parlour and slammed the door in his face.

She paced the room, which was only about ten steps in either direction, muttering to herself. 'Think, woman, think, there must be some way.'

While she walked, she took stock of the room's contents and her eyes alighted on the bottle of wine on the table which remained untouched. It didn't look like the sort of wine she normally drank and was no doubt vinegary, but an idea came to her and she began to smile to herself. Grabbing the bottle, she poured most of the contents onto the meagre fire, which was only spluttering anyway, and the rest into Gervaise's empty ale tankard. That done, she went over to the door and opened it a crack once again.

'Er, excuse me, but could you come and help me with the fire, please? It seems to have gone out,' she said to the tiger, doing her best to appear meek and downcast.

'Fire? It's bleedin' summer!' he replied insolently. 'Shouldn't think as how you need it anyhow.'

'But it's awfully damp in here and I'm

chilled to the bone,' Ianthe insisted. 'Mr Warwycke wouldn't have any use for me if I was to become ill.'

'Well, can't you do it yerself?'

'No, I don't know how. My maid usually does such things for me.'

'The Lord give me strength… Oh, very well,' the youth grumbled and came reluctantly into the room.

Ianthe retreated so that she was standing behind the door as he came in, and the moment he had entered fully, she brought the bottle down on top of his head with as much force as she could muster. It shattered, making an awful racket which had her gasping with fear in case anyone should come running to see what was going on, but it had the desired effect. The tiger crumpled to the floor without a sound. Feeling guilty for hurting the poor youth, even though she had had no choice, Ianthe bent down to make sure he was still alive. To her relief, there was a fairly strong pulse beating underneath his ear, so she was reassured that he was not badly wounded.

Ianthe picked up her skirts and fled. She ran towards the back of the building, rather than the way they had come in, and found herself in a dirty kitchen where two women turned startled eyes on her. Ianthe put her finger to her mouth to keep them quiet, and whispered with a fake smile, 'Shh, please, he likes it when he has to chase me a bit. Spices things up, you know. Don't tell him which way I've gone, then he'll find me too quickly.'

The women looked bemused, but they seemed to accept Ianthe's explanation and didn't say a word. Ianthe darted out through the open door into the back yard and ran as fast as her legs would carry her, through a meadow of sorts and into an area of trees. From there she could see the road by which they had arrived, and she decided her best chance would be to follow that back to where it had divided from the main road. She didn't go onto the road itself, but followed it from within the safety of the trees as no doubt Gervaise would come looking for her as soon as he found her gone. She had no idea how long it would take to walk back to London, but even if she had to keep going all night, she would do so. Anything to escape Gervaise and his evil plans.

Two hours later, Ianthe was still walking and darkness was falling. She had found the main road and thanked her lucky stars that she had paid attention to her surroundings rather than the Misses Gardiner's chatter on the way there. It helped to recognise certain landmarks, so she knew she was on the right track. Fear of pursuit made her turn frequently to scan the road behind her, and whenever anyone approached she hid behind bushes or trees as best she could. Gervaise and his tiny henchman had gone past her twice on horseback, but luckily she had been well concealed behind a thick hedge each time and they hadn't spotted her. She prayed that her luck would hold.

It was fully dark by the time she reached the village of Knightsbridge and knew that she had not much further to go. Despite being used to walking some distance in the country, she was extremely tired, and wanted nothing so much as to be safely home and in bed.

Just as she reached the other side of Knightsbridge, the sound of horses' hooves could be heard behind her again. She looked around wearily for somewhere to hide, but this time she was too late as one of the riders shouted out, 'There she is, after her!'

Ianthe tried to make her tired legs run, but it was a futile effort and she knew it. There was a house up ahead, but in moments her pursuers were upon her and she didn't even make it halfway there. Gervaise grabbed her hair to stop her in her tracks, then jumped down from the saddle, throwing his reins to the tiger, who was astride the other horse. Ianthe cursed her bad luck. If only she had managed to go just a little further, then there would have been people about.

Gervaise turned her round none too gently and shook her like a rag doll. She tried to fight him off, but his anger gave him added strength and she, in contrast, was tired. 'So you thought you could escape, did you? Stupid woman. Come on, you'll have to ride in front of me.'

He pushed her towards the horse, and although she dug her heels in, it was no use. He gave her no chance to escape. Clawing and kicking at him, she screamed for help until he clamped a hand over her mouth. 'Be quiet! No one is going to come to your rescue here anyway. They're used to men from the town coming here with their doxies.'

He swept a contemptuous glance over her clothing, which was now torn and travel-stained, and Ianthe realised that no one would believe her if she claimed to be a lady of birth. Stifling a sob, she bit his hand and screamed again, though she knew it was hopeless, and in response he cuffed her hard before manhandling her up into the saddle.

'Hold her while I mount,' he ordered the

tiger, but before he had time to do so, two more riders came galloping along the road and came to a skidding halt next to them.

'Do you require assistance, Miss?' one of them asked, and Ianthe almost fainted with relief when she recognised the voice.

'Wyckeham,' she cried. 'Oh, please help me. I … he…' She couldn't finish the sentence as tears of relief clogged her throat.

'Ianthe? By all that's holy. What is going on here?'

Gervaise looked stunned for a moment, then he recovered his composure and strived for his usual nonchalant expression. 'The stupid girl wanted an adventure, but now she's getting cold feet. I was just about to take her home, but you may as well spare me the effort if you're going towards London anyway. Here, she's all yours.'

Without further ado, he pulled Ianthe off the horse and mounted it himself in one swift motion. She landed awkwardly, and Wyckeham jumped off his own mount in order to steady her. By the time she had done so, Gervaise and his tiger had ridden off in a cloud of dust.

Ianthe's teeth were chattering now. Wyckeham took off his jacket and draped it round her shoulders. He scowled furiously at her. 'What on earth were you thinking, to go off with that scoundrel? Were you out of your mind?'

'N-no, I didn't … it wasn't like that … you must listen… I…' Ianthe couldn't form a coherent sentence.

'Let's get the poor girl home, Wyckeham. Looks to me as if she's had a nasty shock.' Ianthe looked up at the second rider, whose presence she had forgotten for a moment, and registered the fact that it was the Earl of Somerville.

'Oh, no,' she muttered. It was bad enough for Wyckeham to see her disgrace, but the Earl as well? No doubt the entire town would hear of it now.

Wyckeham nodded and put his arm around her to lead her over to his horse. 'Whatever happened, you can tell us later.

For now, we need to get you home.'

With Somerville's help, he seated her in front of him and mounted behind her, holding on to her with one strong arm. Ianthe buried her face in his shoulder, too exhausted to think for the moment, and she felt his arm tighten around her. 'Rest for a moment, then you can tell us what happened.'

CHAPTER SIX

Wyckeham and Somerville were both staring at her in utter disbelief. 'So you're saying that you were kidnapped by Gervaise, with the help of Robert and your own sister?'

As they rode the last part of the way into London, Ianthe had recovered enough to be able to give them an account of her ordeal, but it did not appear that either of them believed her and her spirits fell even further.

'I swear, it happened just as I've told you, but I don't think Robert or the others had any idea of what was afoot. I really didn't want to get into the phaeton with Mr War-wycke, but it seemed churlish to refuse when Serena had hurt herself, and besides I thought we would all travel close together just as we did on the way there.'

'You are certain your sister was really

injured?' Wyckeham looked very sceptical. 'It all seems rather convenient to Gervaise's plans if you ask me.'

Ianthe didn't reply, but stared at the ground.

'What are you saying, Wyckeham? Are you accusing Miss Templeton of being an accomplice?' Lord Somerville sounded stunned.

'I wouldn't put it past her,' Wyckeham muttered.

'We will have to get to the bottom of this,' the Earl said, his mouth a thin line of disapproval. 'But Miss Templeton has always seemed to me to be a kind, caring person and I cannot believe she would do such a thing.'

Wyckeham sent him a sardonic smile. 'Wearing rose-tinted spectacles, were you, Somerville? Miss Templeton may be beautiful, but even you must have noticed her tendency to want to have her way at all cost?'

The Earl looked slightly sheepish. 'Well, of course, but a woman as beautiful as that is bound to be a little spoiled. I mean, it stands to reason, but *this*,' he waved a hand in Ianthe's direction, 'this goes beyond what is acceptable.'

'Well, we shall see what she has to say shortly.'

Ianthe was relieved that the Marquess said no more. She didn't want to make any direct accusations, since she knew it would be her word against Serena's. Unwittingly, however, her sister gave herself away the moment they were all ushered into the hall, where Serena and her mother were just donning their wraps, ready to go out. Ianthe entered first and Serena caught sight of her.

'You!' she spat, staring daggers at Ianthe. 'What on earth are you doing here? You're supposed to be...'

'Where, exactly?' Wyckeham asked silkily, coming in behind Ianthe. 'With my dear relative Gervaise? Is that what you were going to say?'

'Well, that is who I left her with and he said he'd ... well, never mind that.' Serena was scowling at her sister, oblivious to everyone else. 'I should have known you'd spoil everything as usual.'

'Serena, what is going on here?' Lady Templeton regarded her daughter sternly. 'I thought you said Ianthe had retired with a headache. Are you telling me she never came home with you?'

'No, she wanted to go off with Mr Warwycke so I covered for her.'

'I wanted no such thing,' Ianthe protested. 'I was forced to ride with him because you had hurt your foot – which, I see, seems not to be troubling you now.' Ianthe had noticed her sister was not limping at all.

'You didn't mention you were injured,' Lady Templeton was still frowning.

'It was a mere trifle. Nothing to worry about. Only Mr Warwycke would make a fuss and insist I go in the brougham.'

'Very convenient, and then he drove off with me in his phaeton without waiting for you and the others,' Ianthe said.

Serena shrugged. 'He told me he wanted a

chance to be alone with you. I thought you'd be glad of an admirer. You haven't exactly had them in droves. How was I to know he would take so long to bring you back?'

'He's the last man on earth I would want as an admirer, and well you know it. Besides, he had no intention of bringing me back and you were perfectly aware of that too, I'll wager.'

Serena laughed. 'And what if I was? You should thank me for netting you a husband at last. He'll have to marry you now since you were alone for so long.'

'Of all the under-handed…' Ianthe didn't get a chance to finish her sentence, as the Earl chose this moment to step forward.

'I think you should apologise to your sister at once,' he told Serena. 'You have behaved disgracefully.' She jumped, as she obviously hadn't noticed the Earl's presence behind Wyckeham, and blinked at him stupidly for a moment, but she soon regained her composure.

'My lord, I didn't know you were coming to

fetch us. How v-very kind of you,' she stammered, giving him her best dimpled smile.

He glared at her, seemingly oblivious to her charm for once. 'I came only to escort your sister home,' he said, no trace of his former infatuation in his expression. 'And I'm very glad I did, as I have now seen the true Miss Serena Templeton. You will be relieved to know that henceforth I shall not be troubling you further with my attentions.'

'But, my lord!' Serena looked aghast and hurried forward to put her hands on his sleeve. 'This is all a misunderstanding. I can explain, truly.'

He removed her fingers. 'I don't want to hear it.' He moved over to bow to Ianthe. 'Ma'am, I'm glad Wyckeham and I arrived in time. I shall take my leave now, but I hope to see you out and about again very soon. You can rest assured not a word about this evening will escape my lips.'

'Thank you, my lord, you have been most kind.'

'Not at all, I was happy to be of assistance.' He bowed to the others, but not to Serena. 'Lady Templeton, Wyckeham.'

'But Lord Somerville, I...' Serena tried once more to engage his attention, but he strode out of the house. She stared after him in disbelief, before erupting into a temper tantrum. She whirled on Ianthe and tried to claw her face. 'This is all your fault, you stupid, lying little twit.'

'Enough,' Wyckeham stepped in front of Ianthe, as if to shield her.

'Serena!' Lady Templeton grabbed her daughter's arm at the same instant and pulled her away. 'How dare you! You will go to your room at once and stop this unseemly behaviour. We will speak of this later, but rest assured that your London season is over and your father will be informed immediately. I see now that I have indulged you too much. Well, no more. Now go!'

Shocked by her mother's unusually stern tone and cold words, Serena froze, then turned on her heel and marched up the stairs, still muttering. Silence descended on the hall.

'Would you care for some refreshment, my lord?' Lady Templeton asked Wyckeham, making a visible effort to compose herself.

'Thank you, no, but I think Miss Ianthe may need something. I doubt she's eaten since lunchtime.' He looked at her with concern and Ianthe felt a warm feeling spreading through her as she realised that thanks to Serena's outburst, he now believed her fully.

'I am well enough,' she said gratefully. 'I'd just like to sit down.'

'Then take his lordship up to the drawing room, my dear. I shall ask Cook to prepare something for you.'

Before she had time to protest, Wyckeham picked Ianthe up and carried her up the stairs to the first floor. Once inside the drawing room, he put her down, but he didn't let her go. She stared up into his clear honey-coloured eyes, feeling unaccountably shy all of a sudden.

'I'm so sorry about all this,' she said. 'I'll

quite understand if it's given you a disgust of me and you no longer want to…'

He put a finger on her mouth. 'Shh, you goose. I know it was not your fault – knew it the minute I set eyes on Gervaise, in fact.'

'But you were so angry with me.'

'Not really, it was fear that made me speak that way. I thought for a moment I had lost you to Gervaise, but I should have known you have more sense.' He smiled at her and bent to kiss her.

Ianthe closed her eyes and savoured the feel of his lips on hers. It was wonderful and her whole body melted into his, yearning for more, never wanting it to end. He pulled away all too soon and smiled at her. 'You haven't changed your mind, then?' he asked.

'About what?' Still in a daze, she didn't know to what he was referring at first. 'Oh, no, of course not, but … did you see Papa?'

'Indeed I did, and once I had persuaded him that the rumours about me are untrue, he was very happy to give us his blessing.' Startling Ianthe, he sank onto one knee in

front of her, taking her hand. 'Miss Templeton, will you do me the honour of becoming
my wife?'

Happiness bubbled up inside her. 'Of
course, I would like it very much.'

'That's settled then,' he said and stood up
again, taking her into his arms and kissing
her once more – this time for far longer, but
still not long enough to Ianthe's mind. She
could have gladly stayed in his arms all
night.

Too soon he led her to a sofa and made
her sit down. 'You've had a shock, and we
have all the time in the world to make plans.
For now, I think you should just eat a little,
then go to bed.'

It was only after they had accepted the
rapturous congratulations of Lady Templeton and he had finally taken his leave that
Ianthe realised he still had not said he loved
her.

So why, then, was he marrying her?

The wedding took place only two weeks

later and their whirlwind romance was the talk of the town. Wyckeham obtained a special licence so that they could be married quickly, and Ianthe was happy to go along with his plans. She had never craved a big formal wedding and thought their private ceremony perfect. The fact that Serena had been banished to the country and could not attend made it even better, as far as Ianthe was concerned. She didn't want anything to spoil the day.

If she had any doubts, it was only because Wyckeham had yet to tell her that he loved her, but she reasoned that she was asking too much and just getting along well was enough. He had obviously based his decision on that. After all, hardly anyone married for love; practicality had more to do with it, and there was no doubt that they enjoyed each others' company. Still, she couldn't help but wonder if he would say anything on their wedding night. They had had hardly any time alone before that, as the hasty preparations had filled every waking moment – but once it was all over, they would be together much of the time.

They set off after the reception, and stopped for the night at an inn halfway to Wyckeham Hall. The earl asked for two adjoining rooms and after supper in a private parlour, Ianthe withdrew to prepare for the night. Dupont was with her; as promised, Ianthe had asked her mother if she could take the maid with her and Lady Templeton had been only too pleased.

'You'll need someone you're familiar with, it will help you to adjust to your new circumstances. By all means, take Dupont if she doesn't mind.'

Ianthe entertained a strong suspicion that her mother was being particularly solicitous to try to make up for her previous preoccupation with Serena, although she would never admit as much.

Wyckeham took his time before he finally came to join her and when he did, Ianthe was dismayed to see that he was fully clothed.

'Are ... are you not coming to bed?' she

asked, hardly daring to look at him.

'Not in here, no,' he replied. He made his way over to the bed and sat down next to her, taking one of her hands in his. 'Don't misunderstand me, I would very much like to join you, but I think we ought to get to know one another better first. Everything has been such a rush, don't you think? The last thing I wish to do is to frighten you.'

'I … yes, I suppose you are right.' Ianthe's heart sank. Ostensibly he was being kind, but she couldn't help but think that perhaps he simply was not deeply attracted to her. It seemed obvious, now, that he had married her for convenience only and, although he would have to consummate the marriage at some point in order to beget heirs, he was in no hurry to do so. She reminded herself, however, that she was much better off as his countess than as an unmarried wallflower, so she made an effort to smile at him. 'Goodnight then.'

'Goodnight.' He bent to kiss her cheek, then he was gone.

Wyckeham Hall turned out to be an enormous building made of golden sandstone that shone in the sun as they approached. Ianthe gasped in delight.

'You didn't tell me how beautiful your house is, my lord,' she exclaimed.

Wyckeham smiled. 'It's your house too now, my dear, and did I not ask you to call me Jason?'

'Oh, yes, of course. It's just that it's all so new.'

Ianthe still had trouble believing that he was her husband and that everything he owned was now at her disposal. It was like a fairytale.

'We're nearly there now. Are you ready to meet the staff? No doubt they're lined up and waiting to greet you. I sent word to say that we were coming.'

'I look forward to meeting them.'

'There is one person, however, who doesn't know – Caroline, my sister-in-law. Robert's mother.'

'Oh, how so?'

'Well, I have to confess that I thought it best not to inform her in case she decided to cause a scene at our wedding. She's rather prone to those, unfortunately.'

'But why would she want to do that? I don't understand. Surely, she ought to be happy for you?'

'Well, you see, she's been living here for the last five years and is used to ruling the roost, but as my wife it will be up to you to run the household now, so I rather fear her nose will be put out of joint.'

'Oh, but I wouldn't want to tread on anyone's toes. If she is used to dealing with matters, perhaps it's best to leave it at that? I don't mind, truly.'

'But I do. I want her out of my house and I'd been meaning to ask her to move to the Dower House in any case. But the opportunity had not yet arisen.'

'I'm sure she'll understand, once you explain. After all, offering her a house of her own is very generous of you.'

He smiled. 'Somehow, I doubt she'll see it that way, but I hope you're right.'

Ianthe soon found she wasn't, however. Only moments after they set foot inside the enormous hall, a woman came hurrying down the stairs and in a loud voice that echoed round the marble that was everywhere, she began to berate Wyckeham without bothering to greet him first. Ianthe stared at her, amazed by such blatant rudeness.

'So you've finally deigned to come back, have you?' the woman scolded. 'You've been away an age, and never so much as a tiny letter to let me know how things are progressing. Where is Robert? Have you found him a wife yet? I do hope it's someone suitable and not some impecunious miss with only her pretty face to recommend her. I...'

'Caroline,' Wyckeham interrupted her flow as she came to a halt next to him, 'may I introduce my wife, Ianthe.'

'Your *what?*' Caroline's face went white with shock, then a dusky pink with some emotion that Ianthe could only assume was anger since the woman was scowling mightily.

'My new wife, Caroline. We were married yesterday.'

'But … you? I thought Robert was the one who was supposed to marry, not you. Of all the underhanded, low-down… What do you mean by it?'

Caroline was spluttering, her fists clenching and unclenching at her sides. Ianthe wondered whether she was in danger of an apoplectic fit.

'Mean by it? My dear Caroline, I have a right to fall in love, the same as everyone else, surely?' He glanced at Ianthe as he said this, throwing her into confusion, and she wondered if he meant his words or whether he was only pretending for Caroline's benefit. 'Now, I would be grateful if you would greet my wife in a fitting manner and order us some tea. We're famished.'

'Well, if this isn't the outside of enough.' Without so much as a word to Ianthe,

Caroline marched off, back up the stairs and soon a door could be heard slamming. Ianthe saw several members of staff trying to hide a smile. She decided to proceed as if nothing had happened and turned to greet them, smiling and trying to remember their names. The housekeeper, Mrs Melmoth, was the last person in the line-up, and she curtseyed and smiled. 'May I show your ladyship to your room?'

'Thank you, that would be lovely.'

At least the staff were kind, Ianthe thought to herself as she followed the housekeeper upstairs. But as for Jason's sister-in-law – she simply couldn't believe the woman's conduct. Still, it wasn't her problem and no doubt Jason was more than capable of resolving the situation.

Jason smiled to himself. Caroline's outburst couldn't have come at a more opportune moment, contrasting as it did her behaviour with that of the new marchioness. Ianthe would probably have succeeded in charming the staff in any case, he thought, but Caroline's behaviour made his wife's friendly overtures and kind words even more appreciated. Even Melmoth, the butler and husband of the housekeeper, had deigned to smile and bow low to his new mistress, which was something of a miracle.

As Jason watched his new wife go off with Mrs Melmoth, he couldn't resist ribbing the butler slightly. 'That went well, don't you think, Melmoth?' he commented drily.

'Er, if you say so, my lord.' Melmoth's expression had returned to neutral and Jason grinned at him.

'I thought it best to surprise Mrs Warwycke. At least it has silenced her now for a little while.'

'Not for long, I'll wager,' Melmoth muttered, then coughed as he realised he may have said too much.

Jason laughed. 'No, I'm sure I shall be treated to a scene or two, but rest assured, there will be an end to them soon. Don't think I haven't noticed what's been going on here. I'm sure the staff will be relieved to know that Mrs Warwycke is moving to the Dower House.'

'Yes, my lord, I can't deny that. Now, where would you like your tea?'

'In the library, please. And could you make sure that every member of staff has a glass of champagne with the evening meal to toast my marriage.'

'Very well, my lord, thank you. I'm sure they'll appreciate that.'

As Jason made his way to what was his favourite room of the house, he felt rather pleased with himself. Everything had worked out surprisingly well and now all he had to do was woo his wife properly. She was so young, and he had decided to take things slowly and not initiate her into all her marital duties until he felt she was ready. It seemed only fair to allow her some breathing space and they had all the time in the world, after all.

Still, it was going to be damned difficult to keep his hands off her for any length of time, but he would manage it somehow. He was determined to make this marriage a happy one.

A short while later Ianthe was shown into the library, where Jason and a tea tray awaited her. He smiled ruefully. 'I apologise for the rude reception earlier. I hadn't anticipated that we would have to confront her by the front door.'

'Don't worry, you had warned me and I shan't take any notice. No doubt she'll become used to the situation; it was a shock, that's all.'

'I'm not so sure, but I've told all the staff to take orders from you and no one else, so don't let her try and usurp your role.'

'Are you sure that is wise? Would it not be better for us to share duties at first, while I'm learning the ways of the household?'

He shook his head. 'No, I think a clean break is best. I will tell Caroline tomorrow that she must move to the Dower House within two weeks. I've had it cleaned and made ready. Now, do join me for some tea.

Cook has excelled herself by the looks of things. Then I'll take you on a tour of your new home.'

Ianthe liked the sound of that, very much.

Caroline, however, refused to budge so much as an inch, and short of carrying her out of the house, there was no way of making her move. Wyckeham told her that was exactly what he would do, and simply gave her the date on which she was to leave, no doubt hoping that she would calm down and accept the inevitable sooner or later. Ianthe, however, realised that Caroline wouldn't give in so easily. She began to make trouble in every way, and Ianthe steeled herself for a battle – there was nothing for it but to put up a fight for her rights as chatelaine.

The staff all seemed to be on her side, which helped, but Caroline still interfered wherever she could, trying to wrong-foot Ianthe and questioning her every decision. It didn't help when Wyckeham was called away to one of his other properties to deal with some emergency only a day after their arrival. Ianthe felt very much on her own.

'What on earth do you think you're doing?' Caroline had come sweeping into the small sitting room at the back of the house where Ianthe was sitting writing a letter to her mother. Four spaniels kept her company, two lolling on a settee and the others around her feet. Caroline was regarding the animals with loathing. 'Dogs are not allowed in the house,' she stated.

'They are now. I like dogs and Melmoth said these were house-trained,' Ianthe replied, calmly. She continued to write.

'They're filthy creatures and they shed hair everywhere. Look at that! How could you allow them on the furniture? Have you no sense?'

Ianthe turned to look at the woman and sighed. 'Jason said I could do whatever I liked in this house and I wanted some company. Dogs are such amiable creatures, don't you think? They don't screech at one all the time,' she added pointedly.

'They're not staying, I tell you. It's disgusting and I won't have it. Go on, out with you, out I say!' Caroline flapped her hands at the dogs, trying to shoo them towards the door, but the two by Ianthe's feet half-stood up and growled.

'Oh, for heaven's sake.' Caroline took a step towards the dogs on the settee, who both bared their teeth at her so that she jumped back. She glared at Ianthe. 'You'll pay for this, see if you don't. And I want you gone as well.'

As she slammed out of the room, Ianthe sighed once more. She had a bad feeling about Caroline, and until the woman had left for the Dower House, she wouldn't rest easy.

As word spread about the marriage, Ianthe began to receive calls from neighbours. Although they were friendly enough, she found most of them superficial and not many of them were her own age. When she went to church on the Sunday, however, she finally met someone whose company she truly enjoyed – the vicar's daughter, Harriet Everly.

Harriet seemed shy at first, but as soon as she noticed that Ianthe wasn't high in the instep, she began to chat more and they realised they had a lot in common. 'Do you ride?' Ianthe asked.

'Yes, when I get the chance. We only have one old nag at the moment, and Papa needs him most days.'

'Why don't you come over to the Hall and ride with me? I'm sure there are any number of horses you can borrow, and I'd appreciate the company. Also, I'd like to visit all the tenants on the estate, but without my husband I won't know who anyone is. Perhaps you could help me out? I'm sure you must know everyone hereabouts.'

'I'd be delighted to and I'm sure they would enjoy meeting you too.'

'Excellent, that's settled then. Would tomorrow at ten suit you?'

'I'll be there.'

From then on, they rode out together each morning and Harriet introduced Ianthe to all the local farmers and tradesmen. 'I think they like you,' Harriet said after their first outing together. 'You're not at all condescending, not like that Mrs Warwycke.' She clapped a hand to her mouth. 'I shouldn't have spoken so freely, should I?'

Ianthe smiled. 'Don't worry, I won't tell a soul. And I can assure you I will do everything in my power not to be like her.'

Jason returned at last, and seemed pleased to see his wife.

'I hear you have been making friends,' he said with a smile.

'Yes, but how did you hear?'

'Oh, news travels fast in the country, you must know that. Actually, it was Caroline. She seemed most put out that you've been welcomed so warmly by our neighbours.'

Ianthe shook her head and sighed. 'I can imagine. I'm afraid we haven't been dealing too well together. I'm sorry if I've let you down. I know you would prefer peace in your household.'

He came over and pulled her into his arms, gazing down at her with a serious expression. 'My dear, I know full well that such a thing is not possible with Caroline. We can only hope that she decides to see sense soon when she notices that she is outmanouvred on every flank. I take it the servants are doing your bidding, as I asked them to?'

'Yes, they've been most helpful.' Ianthe was having trouble concentrating on his words, the sensation of being held by him was so overwhelmingly wonderful. She looked up at him and opened her mouth to say something, but he cut her off by kissing her. It was a gentle kiss, as before, but it began to change subtly while his lips moved over hers as if urging her to respond. She did so without thinking, and the kiss deepened. The rest of Ianthe's body felt strangely detached and tingling, and she began to think that the only thing keeping her upright was Jason's arms.

When the kiss came to an end, he smiled at her, and put up a hand to gently caress her cheek. 'Ianthe, I think...'

A knock on the door interrupted him, and he sighed and let go of her before calling out, 'Enter.'

Ianthe sank down onto the nearest chair, her wayward legs still jelly-like.

'I beg your pardon, my lord, but there's an urgent message for you from London.' The butler had entered the room, proffering a silver salver.

'Thank you.' Jason took the letter and slit it open. 'What now, I wonder? Am I never to have any peace?'

Ianthe saw him frown as he read it. 'Is anything amiss?'

Jason's jaw tightened and he nodded. 'Yes, it's Rob. Seems he's got himself into some serious trouble. I must go and rescue him.' He bent to put a hand on her shoulder. 'I'm sorry I have to leave you again so soon. I had hoped ... but it will have to wait. Will you manage?'

Ianthe could see that he was genuinely troubled and wished with all her heart that she could help him. 'I'll be fine,' she said stoutly and he gave her an approving smile.

'That's my girl. I'll be back before you know it and then perhaps we can finally spend some more time together.'

Ianthe felt herself blush. 'That would be most agreeable.'

They were still sleeping in separate rooms, but the power of his kiss had made her hope that this might be about to change. She sighed. *I'll just have to be patient,* she thought.

Robert was a sorry sight when Jason brought him back to the Hall. He had a black eye, a broken wrist and untold bruises all over his body. His mother was, understandably, appalled.

'Robert, dearest! What on earth has happened to you? Who did this? I thought Wyckeham was supposed to look out for you. Some guardian you are,' she spat at Jason.

Robert frowned and winced when that hurt his swollen eye. 'This has nothing to do with Uncle Jason, Mother. You should rather be thanking him. If it wasn't for him, I may not be alive now.'

'Heaven help us! How so?'

'I'd been gambling and I couldn't pay my debts. The people I owed money to hired someone to give me a going-over and they simply wouldn't stop. He came just in time, and now he's paid my dues it won't happen again.' He hung his head in shame. 'I don't know how I'm ever going to repay you, Uncle. I'll have to hand over all the revenues from my estate for the next ten years at least.'

'Surely not! That's ridiculous,' Caroline cut in, not giving Jason the chance to reply. 'Your uncle should have kept you away from gaming halls in the first place. Why didn't you, Jason? I trusted you to look after my boy.'

Jason opened his mouth to defend himself, but Robert jumped in again, glaring at his mother. 'It's not his fault, mother, I wouldn't listen to him. I thought I knew best and there were some people … well, I know now that they are worthless scum.'

'Let's put it all behind us,' said Jason calmly. 'We will draw a line under this and forget it ever happened. As for repayment, forget it also. As long as you've learned your lesson. Come now, it must be time for dinner.'

'I'd better have a tray in my room.' Robert glanced at Ianthe. 'You won't want someone as disgraceful as me at your table, ma'am.'

'Nonsense,' Ianthe smiled and went up to tuck her hand through the crook of his arm. 'Everyone can make mistakes, we're only human. You're welcome at our table any time, isn't that so, Jason?'

'Indeed. Now do as your new Aunt Ianthe tells you and come along.'

'Aunt? You make me sound positively ancient,' Ianthe protested with a laugh. Robert smiled and agreed with her.

'Yes, you're far too young for me to call

you Aunt. It will have to be Ma'am.'

'No, no, just Ianthe will do. There's no need to stand on ceremony. We're family now, are we not?'

Jason sent her a glance filled with gratitude – and perhaps something else, something she had only dared to dream of.

CHAPTER SEVEN

Robert's spirits recovered quickly, and the following day he and Jason decided to accompany Ianthe on her morning ride. Robert looked surprised to see Harriet join them, and Ianthe explained to him about their daily outings.

'Are you sure you don't mind? I can always come back another day,' Harriet said, looking concerned. 'I don't wish to intrude.'

'No, please don't go,' Robert said, going over to help her mount, despite his bandaged wrist. 'I'll feel like the third wheel with these lovebirds otherwise; they'll probably ignore me completely. If you come, I'll have someone to talk to.'

'We would never be that rude,' Wyckeham retorted with a smile, 'but you're very welcome to come along, Miss Everly.'

The tenants they met along the way all greeted Ianthe effusively, and Wyckeham threw her an amused glance. 'You have been busy charming the locals in my absence, I see. Well done!'

Ianthe felt herself blush. 'I hope that was the right thing to do? Only you did say it was best to be on friendly terms with everyone.'

'Of course, and I'm very pleased they like you. It makes life a lot easier.' He glanced over his shoulder to where Robert and Harriet were deep in conversation. 'And I'm glad you've made such a delightful friend. I was afraid you would be a bit lonely here, but you did say you like living in the country.'

'I love it. I couldn't ask for anything more, truly.' Inside, Ianthe thought to herself that there was one more thing she would like, but she mustn't be greedy. No one could have everything they wished for and in time, perhaps Wyckeham would at least come to care for her a little.

'Must we have the vicar to dinner yet again? He and his family were here only last week,' Caroline complained when she heard Ianthe ask Jason if she could invite a few neighbours, including Harriet and her parents. Robert was going back to his own estate the following day, and Jason had reluctantly agreed to accompany him as there were some urgent business matters to discuss there, so Ianthe felt they ought to have a special dinner that evening.

'He's a nice enough fellow,' Jason said, 'and I liked his daughter. Sensible young woman, wouldn't you say, Robert?'

'Oh, yes, a very fine girl indeed, and a bruising rider to boot.'

Jason and Ianthe exchanged an amused glance. It hasn't escaped their notice that Robert had been very taken with Harriet, and Jason had whispered to his wife that Harriet was exactly the sort of girl Rob needed. 'A vast improvement on your sister, with whom he was infatuated for a while, if you don't mind me saying so.'

'Of course not,' Ianthe had smiled. 'I wouldn't wish Serena on anyone half as nice as Robert, and Harriet would make a wonderful wife for any man. Perhaps we could take her with us when we go and visit Robert in the autumn?'

'Excellent idea. Just don't tell his mama, she was hoping for an heiress at the very least for him.'

Jason added now, 'If you don't like the company, Caroline, you don't have to join us. Once you've moved to the Dower House, you can invite whoever you choose to your table.'

Caroline glared at him. 'As I have told you repeatedly, I don't see why I should have to move out. You asked me to come and live here and promised to look after us. Are you breaking your word now?'

'I never said it was to be forever and I think I'm being very magnanimous in offering you a house of your own, free of charge, as well as a monthly allowance. I've already bought your son an entire estate. What more could anyone possibly ask of me?' Jason was frowning now, his good humour evaporated, but Caroline seemed not to notice.

'I call it shabby to evict your own flesh and blood from the family home and I'm sure most people would agree with me. The Hall is big enough to house an army. Why should I have to go and live in that little cottage?'

'Cottage?' Robert spluttered. 'Mother, honestly, you go too far sometimes. It's a six-bedroom house, for heaven's sake, and most agreeable!'

'Well, however large it is, I don't want to live there and don't think you can coerce me into leaving when there is absolutely no need for me to do so.'

'I really think you'll be more comfortable in your own establishment, Caroline–' Jason began, but Robert cut him off brusquely.

'Mother, you are being unbelievably obtuse. There is every need for you to go. This is Uncle Jason's house and as a newly-wed, of course he wishes to be alone with his wife, it stands to reason. Most people would consider that he's being incredibly generous to you, not to mention what he's already done for me. I am vastly indebted to him, while you, on the other hand, are an ingrate. I'm sick and tired of listening to your complaints day in and day out, when you have nothing whatsoever to complain about.

'Now do stop this ridiculous wrangling and do as Uncle says. If you have not moved into the Dower House by next Friday, I shall come and carry you over there myself. Understood?'

Caroline's face turned almost puce with anger and she struggled for words. 'Well, really.' She glared at Jason. 'Now you've managed to turn my own son against me on top of everything else. It's not to be borne.'

'Mother,' Robert scowled and went over to grip her arm, leading her towards the door. 'That's enough now. I'm perfectly capable of forming my own opinions, without being influenced by my uncle, and it's clear as day to anyone with sense that he is being entirely reasonable and you are not.'

'Reasonable? Him? He doesn't know the meaning of the word,' Caroline muttered, but she allowed Robert to tow her to the door. He propelled her bodily through it and closed it behind him, and her voice could be heard echoing down the corridor.

Jason sighed and drew his hand through his hair. 'I'm sorry you had to witness that. She really is impossible.'

Ianthe shook her head. 'Don't worry, I'm sure Robert can calm her down.' She stepped towards him, then stared at the carpet before venturing, 'You know, if you wanted the house to yourself, you could have just moved her out. You didn't have to marry me so that you had a good excuse to do so.'

He put his hand under her chin to lift it so that she had to look at him again. 'Is that what you think? That I married you just for that?'

'I … I don't know, but…'

'I didn't, Ianthe. Believe me, there were other reasons, although I won't deny your arrival has brought this matter to a head.'

She waited for him to say more, but instead he bent to kiss her, enfolding her in his arms. 'I think I can find other uses for you in due course,' he murmured with a smile, and Ianthe felt her stomach flutter as she caught his meaning. 'But right now, I believe you have a dinner to organise? We will discuss this further when I return from Robert's estate.'

Ianthe felt he had dismissed her, and merely nodded before fleeing the room. She didn't understand why he was still keeping her at arm's length, but she would be counting the days until his return when she hoped to change his mind.

On the Friday morning, just before she was due to leave the house, Caroline startled Ianthe by marching into the morning room without knocking, jangling a bunch of keys. The four spaniels lifted their heads and growled simultaneously, but for once Caroline barely glanced at them.

'I suppose you'd better have these,' she

said. 'Not that you'll know what half of them are for.' Ianthe stretched out her hand to take the keys, but Caroline snatched them back. 'Although as I'm not leaving for a little while yet, I could show you if I must.'

Ianthe wasn't sure if this was an olive branch of sorts or just a delaying tactic, but decided she had better accept it just in case. 'That would be kind,' she said. 'Straight away?'

'Why not?'

Caroline virtually frog-marched Ianthe up and down the corridors of the house, fitting keys to locks and explaining why certain cupboards were kept locked, but hardly giving Ianthe a chance to remember it all. Towards the end of the tour, when Ianthe was beginning to tire of this game, Caroline opened a door at the back of the hall and led the way down into the cellar.

'Must we go down here?' Ianthe asked. It seemed cold and damp and she hadn't thought to bring her shawl.

'But of course. The wine is kept here. I'll

show you where the best vintages are, under lock and key of course. It will only take a moment.'

It seemed a long way through winding, dark passages and Ianthe glanced over her shoulder as they walked. They each had a lantern to light the way, but all around them dark shadows encroached. 'It seems very far to go for wine,' Ianthe commented.

'Not at all. Besides, this is it. In here.' Caroline unlocked a door and indicated a large room beyond, with bottles and casks stacked in neat rows around the walls. 'Go on, see for yourself. There are some fabulous vintages.'

Inathe stepped inside, hesitating on the threshold. 'I really don't think...' she began, but before she had time to finish her sentence, Caroline gave her back a shove that sent her stumbling into the room, then she heard the door close and the click of the lock. 'Caroline!' she shouted. 'What on earth are you doing? Stop this at once. Let me out of here!'

But Caroline merely laughed and soon Ianthe could hear the woman's footsteps receding into the distance. An unearthly silence settled on the room, and Ianthe held up her lantern to better inspect her prison.

'Damn her,' she muttered, feeling entirely justified in using such an unladylike expletive. Caroline really was the outside of enough. How long was she planning on keeping Ianthe down here? Long enough to give her a fright, or did she have a much more sinister plan? A shiver coursed through her at the thought that no one else knew she was here.

'Help!' she shouted. 'Somebody, please!' But she knew it was futile. There was no one who could possibly hear her, no one at all.

'Oh, dear God, what am I going to do? Help me, please,' she whispered, and bent her head in prayer.

Ianthe grew steadily colder throughout the afternoon, or what she assumed to be the afternoon as she had no way of telling the time. She tried stamping her feet, jumping up and down and rubbing herself with her hands, but the damp began to penetrate to her very core. She had to find a way out.

At first she focused her efforts on the door, battering it with a stout piece of wood she found on the floor, but it soon splintered and she was still as much of a prisoner as before. Using her shoulders proved painful and no more effective, and a thorough search revealed not so much as a crack of daylight or any other way out. Dejected, Ianthe slumped down upon an upturned cask of port.

'What am I to do?' she whispered, but her only reply was a scurrying noise that came from a corner of the room. She shuddered. 'Ugh, rats.'

As she continued to ponder her situation, however, she suddenly became aware of the fact that she was colder on one side than the other. Cautiously, she held out her hand and detected a flow of air. She jumped up and felt the air before her with her hand, not quite sure what she was looking for, but certain that there was something to be found.

'Eureka!' A slight draught was coming from the wall behind a small tower of casks, and when she walked around them, she put her hands on the wall to feel for any cracks, pushing gently. At first nothing happened, but when she moved fractionally to the left and pushed again, she thought she felt the wall move a little. She gave it an almighty shove and to her delight this entire section of the wall suddenly moved, revealing a large gap behind it, where the air flowed strongly as if driven by wind.

Ianthe had time to see that it was a tunnel, before her lantern chose that moment to splutter and go out, leaving her in almost impenetrable darkness.

Now that she knew there was a possible way out, Ianthe didn't allow the Stygian blackness to overwhelm her. She put out her hands and took a step forward, feeling for the walls on either side, then she began to move cautiously along the tunnel. The floor was rough and uneven and she stumbled a few times, but she continued undaunted, the thought of freedom spurring her on.

The breeze became stronger as she went, making her shiver in her thin gown, and Ianthe tried to walk faster in order to stay warm. She had the feeling she was walking on a downward slope, which felt strangely disorientating in the dark, but at last she began to see a shimmer of light and was able to hurry along until she saw an opening with fading daylight outside. It would seem it was nearly evening.

So happy was she to have found a way out of the cellar, that Ianthe forgot to be careful and as she erupted into what looked like a cave by the seashore, she ran full tilt into a strange man.

'Sacré bleu!' he exclaimed and grabbed her by the arms none too gently. 'Qui êtes vous?'

Ianthe stared at him in shock for a moment, before recovering her composure. She replied in competent French that she was Lady Wyckeham and that he was trespassing on her husband's land. 'Now let me go, sir,' she demanded.

'Nom de Dieu, but I don't think so,' the man muttered, keeping hold of her as he raked her with his eyes from top to toe, making what she assumed to be appreciative noises. A grin spread over his dark features. 'Surely, Madame has time to stay for a short while?'

'No, I don't. Let go of me this instant, or it will be the worse for you.' Ianthe began to struggle, but his grip was impossible to break and when he hauled her up close to his body, one arm snaked around her and held her even tighter. Ianthe tried kicking his shins, twisting and turning, but this only seemed to encourage him.

'I like a woman who fights a little. C'est passionnant.' He chuckled.

Ianthe decided that in that case, the time had come to fight dirty. She had two younger brothers who were boxing enthusiasts, and she had heard them discussing fighting tactics on numerous occasions. Without further ado, she went limp in the man's arms so that he lost his grip slightly, then her hand shot out and she poked him in the eyes with two fingers. He yelled out a curse and let go of her to clutch his eyes. Ianthe didn't wait to see what he would do next. She picked up her skirts and ran.

Her rides with Harriet had taken her to the top of the cliffs once or twice and Ianthe quickly got her bearings, once she had scrambled up the steep path to the top. She thanked her lucky stars that the man had been alone. He had also been rather heavy-set and she had no doubt she could outrun him if she had to. With her heart beating like a demented bird inside a cage, she continued towards the Hall, looking behind her every few seconds to make sure the man wasn't following. Thankfully there was no sign of him.

'My lady! Where have you been? And your gown...' The butler, Melmoth, stared at her in dismay when she barged into the main hall some time later, breathing heavily and sinking onto the nearest chair.

'I ... coast... Frenchman...' she began, then realised she wasn't making sense. She held up a hand and Melmoth waited patiently, looking concerned. 'Is Mrs Warwycke still here or has she gone to the Dower House?' Ianthe asked when she was finally able to speak again.

'Why, she left hours ago, my lady. But I don't understand.'

'No matter, I just wanted to make sure she was gone. This is between you, me and his lordship, Melmoth, but she locked me in the wine cellar.' The butler gasped. 'I don't know how long she intended to keep me there, but it was freezing and I had no food. 'I ... never mind, I found a way out. A secret tunnel that leads down to the coast, to a cave.'

'Ah,' Melmoth said, 'that must be the old smuggler's tunnel. I believed that it had been securely closed up.'

'I think perhaps you ought to see to it. I found a Frenchman in the cave.'

'Surely not!'

'Oh, yes. No doubt about it, but thank God I managed to escape his clutches. I have no idea whether he was a smuggler or a spy, but either way, I wouldn't like to think of him coming into the house in the dead of night.'

'I'll see to it straight away, my lady, but first I'll order you a bath and send for the physician.'

'I'm fine, Melmoth, really, there's no need.'

'Nevertheless, I'm sure his lordship would insist, so if you don't mind, I shall send for the doctor all the same.'

'Very well then, thank you. And remember, not a word to anyone except his lordship of course.'

'You can count on me, my lady.'

'I don't believe it! Of all the ... honestly, Ianthe, if I'd thought her capable of such malice, I never would have left you here alone with her.'

Jason had returned and was pacing up and down next to Ianthe's bed, where she was recovering from her exhausting day. She had had her bath, which helped to thaw out her frozen limbs, and the doctor had been to see her, prescribing bed rest for a day or two.

'But I'm not ill,' she had protested.

'Perhaps not, but you've had a shock and trust me, tomorrow you may feel a trifle unsteady if you don't rest,' the doctor replied. 'It's just a precaution.'

The doctor had been on his way out when Jason arrived home, and Jason had hurried straight up to Ianthe's room, alarmed.

'All is well,' she said now. 'I'm fine, the tunnel has been blocked up and Caroline won't be setting foot in the house for quite a while if I know Melmoth.' She smiled. 'He can be very fierce when he wants to.'

He grinned back. 'Don't I know it, but in this instance I'm glad of it. If I have to set eyes on that woman again this side of Christmas, I'll probably wring her scrawny neck.

I'm very tempted to cut off her allowance altogether.'

'No, please don't do that – she'll only come and pester us and in all honesty I'd rather not see her again either.'

'You're right, of course.' He came to sit on her bed and took her hands in his. 'I was looking forward to spending some time with just you for a change, but I suppose that will have to wait a day or two now.'

'I'll be as right as rain by tomorrow,' she said quickly. 'Perhaps we can have dinner for two then?' She felt herself blush at her own boldness, but throughout the long hours in the cellar her thoughts had kept returning to her husband and she had been distraught to think that she might never see him again. Now he was here – and she knew that she had to try and make him love her somehow. She couldn't bear it if he didn't.

He kissed each of her hands in turn and smiled. 'That sounds like a good plan. I shall look forward to it.'

After a good night's sleep, Ianthe saw no reason why she should stay in bed, but she rose much later than usual and when she sat down to breakfast, Melmoth informed her that Jason had already gone out for a ride.

'Just left a moment ago, my lady. I'm sorry, but I believe he thought you would be resting today, else I'm sure he would have waited for you.'

'Yes, well, I probably ought to take it easy. I'll just go and write some letters or read a book, I think.'

She had barely sat down at her desk, however, surrounded as usual by her canine companions, when Melmoth knocked on the door to announce that she had a visitor. 'I've put him in the blue salon, my lady. It's his lordship's ramshackle relative, Mr Warwycke.'

'Robert? But I thought…'

'No, the other one. Mr Gervaise.'

'What?' Ianthe frowned. How dare he show his face here after what he had done? Anger surged through her momentarily, then she took a deep breath. 'Very well, I'll go and see what he wants here, but please stand by in case I need assistance.'

Gervaise was lounging by the French doors that opened onto the vast expanse of lawn at the back of the house, and turned with a sardonic smile when she entered. 'Well, well, quite the grand lady now, aren't you,' he mocked, looking her fashionable morning dress up and down. 'No more out-moded gowns, eh? Looks like country life suits you. Are you breeding yet?'

Ianthe gasped at such crudeness. 'That is none of your business,' she said. 'What do you want? Why have you come here?'

'Came to visit my relatives, of course, offer my felicitations, that sort of thing. Isn't that allowed?' He smirked and Ianthe felt like hitting him to wipe the smug expression off his face.

'I doubt you're very welcome here, after what you did to both myself and Robert. If I were you, I'd leave now, before Jason re-turns and finds you in his house. He won't be best pleased.'

'I expect you're right.' Gervaise gave an exaggerated sigh. 'But before I go, could you just tell me what that is? I simply can't make it out.' He pointed to something outside.

'What?' Ianthe came forward to stand beside him and craned her neck, but there was nothing out of the ordinary. 'I can't see anything…' she began, but her words were cut off and turned into a gasp of indignation as Gervaise's arms snaked round her and twisted her arms up behind her back before she could so much as blink. She realised he had tricked her, and anger flooded her once more. 'No! What are you doing? Let go, this instant.' She tried to fight him off, kicking at his shins, but her thin slippers had little effect and besides, he side-stepped her attempted attack easily while holding on to both her slim wrists with one strong hand. In the next instant, he produced a small, but lethal-looking, knife from his coat pocket and she stopped struggling instantly at the sight of it.

'Don't make a sound if you know what's good for you,' he warned. 'One peep out of you and you'll be no more.' His tone of voice was deadly and Ianthe felt a chill snake down her back, freezing her into immobility as the menace implied in his words registered.

'Now, if you would be so kind as to come with me?' he added, opening the French doors. 'We are going for a little walk in the garden.'

'But I...' Ianthe was about to protest that she would need to change her shoes, then thought better of it as he brandished the knife.

'Put your hand on my arm as if we are walking companionably and go, or you'll feel the point of this,' he hissed.

Ianthe had no choice but to obey. There was no doubt that he was in earnest and she didn't wish to antagonise him. If she cried out for help, Melmoth would come to her rescue, but by then it may be too late. She simply couldn't risk it. Somehow, she made her feet move forward, one after the other, even though her whole being was focused on that sharp knife, hidden by his hand and aimed at her. *Oh, dear Lord, help me please,* she prayed silently. *I don't want to die now!*

The French doors led onto a wide terrace, with steps down to the lawn and rose garden beyond. They stepped outside, Gervaise taking care to close the doors as quietly as possible behind them. 'This way,' he whispered and led her to the left, pausing at the top of the stairs to look around for a moment, presumably making sure that no one else was about.

Ianthe shivered, although not from cold. Thankfully, she was wearing a spencer since she had been feeling chilly that morning.

'Let's go,' Gervaise said quietly, but just before she could begin to descend the stairs, he gave her a hard push so that she almost lost her balance and thought she was going to tumble down, head first on the hard stone steps. At the very last moment, he pulled her back to safety, then chuckled at her gasp of fear. 'No tricks now,' he warned, 'or you'll go the way of Jason's first wife.'

Thoughts of Elizabeth whirled through her head and Gervaise chuckled again. 'Did you think I was going to finish you off as well?' he asked. 'Not quite yet, my sweet. I have other plans for you first.'

'As … as well?' she stammered, turning to stare at him with horror.

He shrugged. 'Elizabeth was a nuisance and Jason ought to have been grateful to me for getting rid of her.'

Ianthe couldn't help asking, 'But why? I mean, why you?'

'We had been having an affair, but I had tired of her. Elizabeth threatened to tell Jason, who was at that time paying me a meagre monthly allowance which I couldn't do without. The stupid woman.'

Ianthe clamped her mouth shut. She didn't want to know any further details. It was clear to her now that she was dealing with a very dangerous man, possibly even deranged, and if she was to have any chance of survival, she needed to keep all her wits about her.

Gervaise said no more, simply marched her down the stairs and across to the rose garden. A gardener was pruning nearby, but Ianthe managed to smile and nod at him as if nothing was wrong. 'Good girl,' Gervaise hissed. 'Keep going, a little faster if you please.'

'Wh-where are we going?'

'To France,' he said. 'After we have made a few deliveries along the coast.'

'What? But why?'

'I have some business to see to in France, but before that I need to get rid of the smuggled goods I was going to leave in the cellar – which thanks to you,' he scowled at this point, 'I will no longer be able to use as a hiding place.'

'That is not my fault, surely?'

'If you hadn't found the secret passage, it wouldn't now be boarded up, would it?' he sneered. 'Meddling females, can't leave anything alone.'

'Well, I had to find a way out. Caroline had locked me in.'

'She would have told someone eventually. She may be stupid, but she's not capable of killing anyone.'

'Did … did she know about your, er … activities?'

'Yes. She received her share of the profits for turning a blind eye and helping to deceive the Revenue men if they came looking. Not that they did; we only move the goods on nights when we know they're elsewhere. With the cave at the end of that tunnel, it was easy enough to do. Don't know why the foolish woman had to go and lock you in there, of all places, but then using her brain isn't one of Caroline's strong points. Now stop talking and move. I thought you'd like the prospect of a little trip to France, seeing as your French is so good.'

'How do you know that?'

'Oh, my friend told me you had no difficulty understanding him yesterday. He only thought it a shame that you gave him the slip. Don't think you can bamboozle me as easily, though. And unless you want to be doxy to the whole crew, I'd suggest you be nice to me. Extremely nice,' he purred, making Ianthe shudder. 'That way I might only share you with my friend.'

'You're despicable,' Ianthe hissed and tried to pull away from him, but once again she felt the sharpness of the blade on her side and knew he had the upper hand. At least for now.

When Jason returned from his ride, Melmoth was hovering anxiously in the hallway, looking unsure what to do. This was so unusual for the normally unflappable butler that Jason stopped in his tracks. 'What's the matter?'

'It's her ladyship, my lord. She's been in there,' Melmoth nodded towards the blue salon, 'for nigh on two hours now, closeted with your relative, that Mr Gervaise.'

'You cannot be serious? Alone?'

Melmoth nodded miserably. 'She said it

was fine, she would deal with him, and I haven't heard any sounds of an altercation, but...'

Jason marched over to the door of the blue salon and threw it open. He looked inside, then turned in confusion to Melmoth. 'There is no one in there.'

'I beg your pardon? But ... oh.' Melmoth rushed into the room, closely followed by Jason, and both of them came to a halt by the French doors. Jason tried one, and it wasn't locked.

'They must have gone outside, my lord. But why?'

'If I know Gervaise, he's up to no good again. Ianthe wouldn't go for a walk with him willingly. Damn! What does he want with my wife?'

But Jason was afraid he knew the answer to that question all too well. 'Melmoth, assemble all the staff in the kitchen – and I mean everyone, both inside and out. I'll need to speak to them. Someone must have seen something.'

'At once, my lord.'

No sooner had the butler left the room, however, than he returned again, looking puzzled.

'Yes, what is it?' Jason knew he sounded brusque, but he couldn't help it. Worry about Ianthe was gnawing at his insides; he wanted to begin searching for her immediately.

'I'm sorry, my lord, but Mr Gervaise is here again – to see you. I've put him in the library.'

'Gervaise?' Jason was astonished at this turn of events. Had they misjudged the man? 'Very well, I'll see him now. Please go ahead and assemble the staff in the meantime, I still want to speak to them.'

'Very good, my lord.'

Jason swept into the library, prey to conflicting emotions. If Gervaise had abducted his wife, he had a nerve coming back to the Hall. Unless he was going to attempt blackmail? On the other hand, he may be innocent and some other calamity had befallen Ianthe. Had that wretched French-man returned? Perhaps he ought to have had the grounds searched the day before, but he had assumed the man to be long gone. Or had Caroline been up to further mischief? He made a mental note to find out her whereabouts this morning, in case she had.

Gervaise was lounging in a chair by the fireplace, but stood up when Jason entered the room. He looked as if he hadn't a care in the world and Jason felt a momentary urge to punch the man. Instead he took a deep breath and strode forward, coming to a halt in front of Gervaise.

'How dare you set foot in my house again? I understand you came here earlier and spoke to my wife. I doubt she was pleased to see you.'

'On the contrary, dear cousin. Your wife is a very well-bred female, polite to guests, even unwelcome ones, and when I pointed out to her that we are now related and ought not to be at loggerheads, she agreed to a truce. As a matter of fact, we went for a stroll in the garden and then she said she had some business to see to, so I wandered on by myself. Your estimable butler said you wouldn't be back for some time, so I thought I would wait outside as it's such a fine day.'

'You've been in the garden all morning?'

'But of course, isn't that what I just said?' Gervaise gave Jason a smile, but it didn't reach his eyes. Jason thought to himself that Gervaise's smiles never did. They were as false as the man himself, but for now, he decided to play along.

'I see. Very well, then, tell me why you have come. I may safely assume that this is not a social visit?'

'Ever the affable host,' Gervaise sneered.

'Gervaise, I've had a very trying morning. What do you want?'

'A small loan. Say, five thousand? I'll pay it back. I'll even write you an IOU if you wish.'

Jason stared at his relative, amazed by the effrontery of the man. Quite apart from the fact that he had tried to kidnap Jason's wife in London, he had led Robert astray and almost got him killed. 'You speak in jest, surely?'

'No, it's not a joking matter.'

'Damn right, it isn't.' Jason shook his head. 'Gervaise, I'm not giving you another penny. Ever. You almost lost me my nephew and I didn't for a moment believe your tale regarding that picnic with Ianthe and her sister, so how you can possibly think I'd lend you any money is beyond me. Now kindly leave my house and don't return.'

Gervaise appeared about to argue, then thought better of it. 'Gracious, as always. Very well, so be it. Adieu, dear cousin. Don't worry, I'll see myself out.'

As Gervaise strolled to the door, Jason had the urge to run after him and beat him to a pulp, but he restrained himself and waited until he heard the front door slam before calling for Melmoth.

'Have him followed,' he ordered. 'I don't trust him and I still haven't ruled out his involvement in her ladyship's disappearance.'

A short time later Jason stood in the huge kitchen, surrounded by every one of his servants. Fear gripped his stomach as he thought of Ianthe, either at the mercy of Gervaise once again or someone else equally ruthless, but he quashed these thoughts and held up his hands to gain everyone's attention.

'I am sorry to say that my wife has gone missing. Has any one of you seen her about today?'

One of the gardeners raised a hand. 'I did, sir. She were walking in the rose garden with a gentleman. Smiled at me kindly, she did.'

'And when was that?'

'Oh, a while ago now, my lord. Seemed in a bit of a hurry, if you know what I mean. Usually, she stops to smell some of the blooms, but not today.'

'What did the gentleman look like, do you remember?'

'Er, a bit like yourself, sir, only smaller and

with a bright yellow waistcoat.'

Gervaise had been wearing a yellow waist-coat, Jason thought to himself, and there was a certain family resemblance between them, but this only proved that he had walked in the garden with Ianthe like he claimed – and not that he had then abducted her.

'In which direction were they heading.'

'Dunno, sir. Just wanderin', I s'pose.'

'And did you see her return?'

'No, m'lord.'

'Right, thank you. Did anyone else see them?'

No one spoke up. Jason wanted to shout with frustration. Gervaise may have forced Ianthe to go with him, but where could he have taken her? If he'd had a carriage waiting somewhere, she could be long gone. Or might she simply have fallen and hurt herself? Perhaps she was, even now, lying helpless in the grounds somewhere?

'We'll need to organise search parties and see if we can find any clue as to where she went after leaving the rose garden. Let's have four teams, please, one for each direction and...'

'My lord?'

'Yes?' Jason looked impatiently in the direction of Ianthe's French maid, Dupont, who was holding up her hand.

'Why you not use the dogs?'

'Dogs? Yes, of course. Carter,' he turned to the man in charge of his hunting pack, 'go and...'

'No, milord,' Duont interrupted him. 'I mean les épagneules. They like 'er ladyship, they may follow 'er.'

'Ep–...? Oh, the spaniels! Of course, why didn't I think of that? Thank you. Melmoth, where are they?'

'I expect they're still in the morning room. They were keeping her ladyship company earlier.'

'Fetch them, please, someone. And Dupont, could you find a piece of clothing my wife has worn recently? Let's see if the dogs can track her. In the meantime, the rest of you may as well search the gardens.

There may be some clue that will help us.'

One of the footmen came rushing in, out of breath, and Melmoth ushered him forward. 'This is the lad I sent after Mr Gervaise, my lord.'

'Ah, yes, so where did he go? Did you manage to follow him?'

'Yes,' the young man panted, 'went to the inn … in the village … sittin' in the tap room now, he is.'

'I see.' This was not what Jason had hoped to hear. If Gervaise was hanging around the local inn, it seemed unlikely that he had abducted Ianthe after all. Surely he would have set off immediately if that had been the case? He sighed and ran a hand through his hair. 'Very well, we'll have to continue our search. The spaniels, please, Melmoth. The rest of you, go!'

Everyone ran off to do his bidding and Jason went to wait impatiently in the hall for Dupont and the dogs. He prayed that it would work. Failure to find Ianthe was not to be contemplated.

The dogs had never been trained to search and find, but when they were led to the French windows and made to sniff a piece of Ianthe's clothing, they barked excitedly, straining at their leads.

'Where is she? Where's your mistress? Go seek, find her!' Jason egged them on, hoping they would understand. Their tails were wagging frantically, but he wasn't sure if they were merely happy at the prospect of going out into the garden. He, Melmoth and two of the footmen followed the dogs, making them sniff the item of clothing from time to time. When they turned left down the stairs and headed straight for the rose garden, noses to the ground, Jason wanted to shout with joy, but he knew it was too soon. It could be coincidence.

Through the rose garden they went, at great speed, and on the other side of it, the dogs sniffed around some more, then headed off to the right.

'Where are they taking us?' Melmoth

huffed, trying to keep up. Jason hoped the rapid pace would not prove too much for the old man; he was not as fit as he had used to be.

'I'm not sure, but it's not towards the road anyway, which is a relief. If they were on foot, we stand a much better chance of finding them. We'll just have to wait and see. Do you want to rest for a while and catch up with us later?'

'No, I'll be fine, my lord. I can manage, for her ladyship's sake.'

Melmoth looked as determined as Jason felt, and it pleased him that Ianthe had won the respect and loyalty of his servants already. But what good was that if she never came back? He pushed that thought to the back of his mind, refusing to even con-template such a thing.

I have to find her, for everyone's sake. No, that's a lie – I want to find her for myself. Ianthe's disappearance had made him realise just how precious she was to him. If anything happened to her, he would never forgive himself. Having found her, how could he live without her?

It dawned on him that he loved her deeply, and this time it wasn't calf love, like his feelings for Elizabeth. It was the true and abiding kind.

'We must find her,' he muttered.

Melmoth nodded. 'Don't worry, my lord, we will.'

Jason wished he could be as certain.

CHAPTER EIGHT

Ianthe leaned her head back against the hard wall of the little fisherman's hut Gervaise had taken her to and tried to come up with a plan of escape, but nothing came to mind. There were ten men sitting around looking bored, but every time she moved so much as a muscle, at least one of them turned to look at her. It was impossible.

She had never been to this part of the coast before, and it had been quite a trek from the house, especially in flimsy slippers. Her feet ached now, but in the scheme of things it was a minor discomfort. The old hut was near a cove, similar to the one where the cave was, but smaller, and Ianthe could hear the waves caressing the shore below. The noise was soothing, but she still felt on edge.

Gervaise had gone out, soon after their arrival, telling the men not to touch so much as a hair on her head. 'She's mine, understand?' Everyone had nodded in sullen agreement. It would seem that no one argued with Gervaise and Ianthe could only be thankful for that.

She had no idea how long she sat there waiting, but at last Gervaise came back, seemingly in a good mood. 'All well?' he asked the leader of the men, the Frenchman whom Ianthe had had the misfortune to run into the day before.

'Oui, tout va bien.'

'Excellent. Shouldn't be too long now. I'm expecting the ship just after nightfall.' Another man came staggering into the hut, laden with two sacks, and Gervaise turned to indicate him. 'We've brought some victuals from the inn. Tuck in, everyone, you'll need your strength later.'

He helped himself to some bread and cheese out of one of the sacks and brought some over to Ianthe.

'Hungry?' he asked, but she turned her head away.

'No, thank you.'

'Still sulking, are we?' He laughed. 'You'll soon get over it. Once we're in France, I expect you'll change your tune. By then you'll have realised you have to be nice to me unless you want that lot,' he indicated the others with a nod in their direction, 'to enjoy your favours.'

Ianthe shuddered at the thought, but kept her gaze resolutely turned away and her mouth shut. There seemed no point in arguing with him. She simply had to find a way to escape. The alternative didn't bear thinking about.

'Suit yourself,' he muttered and walked away again to join his men, who were now passing round a keg of ale.

Ianthe closed her eyes and waited.

The dogs carried on at the same break-neck pace and Jason had to pull hard on the leads to stop them several times so that Melmoth and the others could keep up. The butler was rather red in the face, but he continued to refuse to be left behind, so after short breaks, they continued on.

'You don't think they're just looking for rabbits?' Melmoth wheezed at one point, but Jason shook his head.

'No, if they were, they'd all be off in different directions like they normally are. It looks to me as though they're following the same trail. Seems we're heading for the coast at the very edge of Wyckeham land.'

'The old cove, do you think?' Melmoth said.

'Possibly. Perhaps I ought to go on alone, just in case? The dogs might bark otherwise and alert people to our presence. If Ianthe is being held against her will, it would be much better to surprise her captors.'

'Yes, but take young Lynch with you, my lord. You shouldn't go alone. And young Jackson, too, perhaps.'

Lynch was the brawniest-looking of the two footmen, and Jackson, although young, looked as if he could handle himself in a fight nonetheless. Jason nodded. 'Very well. You stay here with the dogs then, Melmoth.'

Jason hardly ever came to this part of his estate as there was nothing there apart from an old path running along the top of the cliffs, but he knew every inch of it just the same. 'There is a small thicket of trees and bushes not too far from the cove,' he said to the two men, as they continued on together. 'We should be able to reach that without being seen by anyone, but after that we'll need to proceed far more cautiously.'

They hurried along and were soon enveloped in the welcome cover of leaves and other foliage. The trees here had been planted as a windbreak and Jason was thankful for that now, since it gave them the opportunity to observe any comings and goings to the cove without being seen themselves.

'Let's lie down here for a while. Keep your eyes and ears open, men.'

They dropped to the ground and waited. Over to their right was an old fisherman's hut which was so dilapidated that no one lived in it any longer. Jason had been meaning to have it knocked down, but had forgotten about it. It looked in even worse condition than last time he had seen it, and he paid it scant attention, but after a while, to his surprise, two men came out of the door, one obviously giving orders to the other. Their voices were perfectly audible, carried on the wind and although they were speaking French, Jason had no trouble understanding them. He had had a French grandmother who refused to speak to him in English, thus unwittingly doing him a favour.

'We leave as soon as the tide turns,' the larger of the two men said. 'We should be safe enough here until then, but be on your guard. I don't want any mistakes now, is that clear? You know what you have to do?'

There was a murmur of consent.

'Good. We won't bring the woman until the last minute. Don't want any trouble with her high-and-mightiness and after yesterday, I'm not taking any chances. My eyes are still sore. Monsieur Warwycke said we can't touch her anyway. He wants her for himself, but not until we get there and he has more time for such sport.' The man spat on the ground. 'He is welcome to her. I'll have her when he's tamed her. Now, let's go down to the cove.'

Jason waited until they had disappeared, then signalled for the others to withdraw further into the thicket for a moment.

'Aren't we staying to see if her ladyship is in there?' Lynch looked confused.

'She is,' Jason replied.

'Is that what they said?'

'Among other things. The most important part was that they're leaving with the tide, which won't be until after dark, so we have some time to arrange a little surprise for them. Does either of you have the strength to run to the Excise man's house in the next village?'

'I do, my lord,' Jackson volunteered. 'I can go further yet than that if you require me to.'

'No, that will be enough. Just tell him what I just told you. He'll need to gather his men and head for the cove by sea, but his boats mustn't be seen until Gervaise's ship has entered the cove, understand? It will be dark by then, so it shouldn't be too difficult for them to hide nearby. Lynch and I will stay here to make sure they don't take my wife anywhere else in the meantime. Hurry now.'

'Very good, my lord.'

'Off you go then.'

Jason thought for a moment about what he had overheard. He was sure that Ianthe was in that hut, but although his first impulse had been to rush in and free her, he had no idea how many men were in there with her and it would be foolish in the extreme to attempt a rescue mission without knowing the odds. It would seem she was safe for now, and he could only hope she would remain so. He needed back-up, and he needed it fast.

'Lynch, could you just run back to Melmoth and tell him what we're doing? Ask him to go back to the Hall and send some more men over here as well, please. The more, the better.'

'Will do, my lord.'

Jason returned to keep a look-out, praying as he had never prayed before for his wife to be safe.

As soon as darkness fell, Gervaise and his men began to prepare themselves for the journey. The goods they were taking with them were stacked in piles near the door of the hut, and the moment the signal came from the ship outside, they lined up, each to carry their share. It seemed to Ianthe that they got the job done incredibly quickly, but then she supposed they didn't want to hang around in case they were caught.

Soon, the little dwelling was empty and Gervaise returned for her. He pulled her up and tugged her towards the path down to the cove. She was grateful that he hadn't thought it necessary to tie her up, and wondered if there would be any chance of escaping now. She was a reasonably good swimmer, and jumping overboard seemed like a good alternative to going anywhere with Gervaise.

Unfortunately, it was as if he could read her thoughts, because he produced a length of rope and proceeded to bind her hands in front of her when they reached the tiny beach. 'Just a precaution, you understand,' he smirked. 'Don't want you to get any ideas.'

'You're despicable,' she muttered, testing her bonds to see whether there was any give, but sadly she found that they didn't budge an inch.

'So you keep telling me.' He chuckled. 'Don't worry, I won't hold it against you once you give in to me.'

'I will never do that voluntarily,' she vowed, but infuriatingly, he just chuckled some more and led her over to the waiting row boat.

Lynch had returned with ten strong men, and they had all settled down to bide their time. 'We'll attack when they take her ladyship down to the shore,' Jason decided. From what the Frenchmen had said, he knew that Gervaise was keeping Ianthe safe until they reached France, so there was no need to worry about her yet. 'Better to surprise them in the dark, then they won't know how many of us there are.'

The minute Gervaise led Ianthe out of the hut, Jason gave the signal to his men and they all crept forward and set off down to the cove, trying to make as little noise as possible. Jason was in the lead and heard the exchange between his cousin and Ianthe, which made him smile despite everything. His wife certainly had spirit, he had to admit, and his heart swelled with pride and love. Only a few more moments now, and she would be safe again.

Only half of Gervaise's men were still on the beach when the attack came and pandemonium broke out all around them. Gervaise swore and yanked Ianthe in front of him as a human shield, even though she struggled to escape his grip, kicking and biting him as best she could. He continued to try to pull her in the direction of the row boat, but she dug in her heels to delay their departure.

There were sounds of fighting all around them and grunts of pain, as well as the odd scream indicating serious injury, but to Ianthe's dismay, Jason was prevented from coming straight to her side by the large Frenchman she had bested the day before. A brief struggle ensued, but when Lynch came to his master's aid, they soon had the Frenchman sprawled on the shingle.

'Give up, Gervaise, you're outnumbered,' Jason shouted over the din, but to Ianthe's horror, the man behind her only laughed.

'If you come even a step closer, she dies, cousin,' he drawled, once more producing his knife which glinted in the faint moonlight. 'I mean it. I've killed one of your wives already, it won't bother me to dispatch this one to hell as well.'

'You son of a...'

'Call your men off now, do you hear? We're leaving.'

Reluctantly, Jason did as he was bid and the fighting ceased.

'Don't think you'll get away with this, Gervaise. I'll find you, if it's the last thing I do,' Jason threatened. Gervaise ignored his cousin and bundled Ianthe into the boat. Those of his men who were still standing scrambled in after them.

Ianthe blinked away tears as she watched Jason and the shore recede into the distance while two oarsmen quickly sculled them out to a larger ship which was waiting in the narrow bay that presumably belonged to Wyckeham Hall. Ianthe was forced to climb a rope ladder, while Gervaise pushed from below, obviously relishing this task judging by his continued laughter. At last, she made it onto the deck, and walked quickly to one side, wondering whether she might be able to swim with her hands tied. It might be possible, but if her dress dragged her down, she would be unable to remove it and she might drown. She swore inwardly.

'Come, I'll take you to the cabin,' Gervaise said, and they began to move towards the back of the ship. There were no lanterns to guide them; Ianthe assumed this was because they didn't want to be seen by any Revenue cutters. She stumbled several times on huge coils of rope and other sailing paraphernalia on deck, but Gervaise hung onto her arm to steady her.

Just as they reached what must be the opening to the cabins, a shot rang out, however, and there was suddenly light coming from the mouth of the bay. 'What the...? Damn!' Gervaise pulled her quickly against him, and brought the knife out of his pocket yet again. Ianthe drew in a hasty breath.

'What do we do, sir?'

'It's the Excise men, sir!'

There were shouts coming from all directions and Ianthe heard several splashes as some of the men obviously thought it better to make a run for it than to stay and face the law. Gervaise, however, stood his ground, hanging onto Ianthe for dear life.

'Don't panic!' he shouted to his men. 'We have something to bargain with.' And he pushed and pulled Ianthe towards the railing of the ship so that she could be seen by anyone approaching. As soon as one of the two cutters came alongside them, Gervaise called over to them. 'Let us be on our way or Lady Wyckeham will die. I mean it.'

Ianthe squinted against the light coming from the other ship and couldn't make out how many men it was carrying, nor any other detail, but she recognised the voice that came echoing back cross the water instantly.

'If you touch so much as a hair on her head, you're the one who is going to die, Gervaise.'

'Jason.' Ianthe couldn't believe it. How had her husband managed to get on board the revenue cutter so quickly? She could only assume there had been another row boat nearby waiting to take him to the ship.

'I'm here, my love. Stay calm.'

'How very touching, to be sure,' Gervaise drawled. 'But in case you hadn't noticed, I still have a very lethal knife here and unless you allow us to leave this bay, you will be a widower again, dear cousin, as I said. What do you think the town will make of that, eh?'

'And you'll be a dead man soon after,' Jason growled, but Gervaise merely laughed. 'Admit it, you want me to kill this wife for you as well. Tired of her already, are you? Your infatuations never last long.'

'Why, you whoreson, I'll...'

There came the sound of a scuffle, and one of the excise men began to speak instead. 'You are surrounded and you cannot possibly hope to gain any advantage by killing a lady. If anything, that will make things worse for you all. Give her up, and let us come to some agreement. I'm coming aboard.'

'No, absolutely not. We are leaving now and if you try to stop us, Lady Wyckeham dies. That's all there is to it.'

Ianthe felt her last hope of rescue fade away, but then she realised that if Jason and the others couldn't help her, then it was up to her to do something. Now that they were so close, surely they would be able to save her from drowning if she tried to swim for it? She decided she had nothing to lose by trying. If she stayed, she would die anyway or suffer a fate worse than death.

Taking Gervaise by surprise, she turned suddenly and head-butted him square on the nose, exactly the way her brothers had taught her in the manner of the famous pugilists they so admired. There was a satisfying crunching noise and a yelp of agony from Gervaise, who let go of Ianthe for a moment to clutch his nose. Her forehead hurt, too, but she ignored this minor irritation and scrambled over the railing in a flash. As she jumped, she shouted loudly, 'Get me out of the water, Jason, now!'

In the next instant, the freezing cold sea closed over her head and she went rigid with shock before she remembered she needed to kick out hard in order to return to the surface. It seemed an age before she emerged, coughing and spluttering, but by then she was able to move properly again and she began to swim with a motion resembling doggy paddle. Her skirts were heavy, and the spencer didn't help, but with a great deal of effort she managed to stay afloat.

'Ianthe! Where are you?'

She heard Jason, and called out, 'Over here. Hurry, please!' She was tiring fast and the water seemed intent on dragging her down.

Just when she thought she would be unable to keep afloat for a moment longer, a row boat came into view and hands stretched down to pull her out of the sea. Someone wrapped her quickly in a rough blanket, and then, oh joy! she was in Jason's arms.

'Ianthe, my love, are you all right? Did he hurt you?'

'N-no, I'm f-fine.' She was shivering uncontrollably and her teeth were chattering so much that it was quite difficult to speak. 'Th-thank you for coming to m-my rescue.'

'You did it all yourself. I was at my wit's end. That was very brave of you, if a touch foolhardy.'

He was holding her tight, stroking her back and kissing her temple, her cheek, her nose. She turned her face up and received a proper kiss, an infinitely more satisfying one, that seemed to go on for ever and which she returned measure for measure. This had the effect of warming her right down to her toes and the shivering lessened almost immediately.

'I couldn't have jumped without knowing you were there, though. I knew my skirts were too heavy so I would never have made it to shore. I thought about it earlier, but decided I couldn't risk it.'

'No, I realise that. Well, the main thing is that you are safe.'

The sound of gunfire could now be heard all around them and Ianthe tried to peer through the darkness. 'What is happening?'

'I think Gervaise and his men will find themselves either captive or shot very soon,' Jason said grimly. 'Now that you are no longer on board, the excise men are able to attack without fear of hurting you. Don't think about it any more, we must get you home and into a hot bath. Being frozen twice in as many days cannot be good for you.'

She snuggled up to him, not feeling particularly cold at that moment. 'I'll be fine,' she murmured.

Some time later, Ianthe was back in her bed, bathed and warmed both by blankets and by a medicinal glass of brandy. Jason came in and dismissed the maids, seating himself on the edge of her bed once more.

'I seem to be forever perching here,' he said wryly. 'Perhaps one of these days you'll stop getting into scrapes so that we can have a civilised conversation somewhere else.'

'I'll do my best not to be abducted for a while.' She smiled at him. 'Thank you again for coming to find me. It was lucky you overheard Gervaise's plans.'

'Indeed. The alternative doesn't bear thinking of.' He put out a hand to stroke her cheek. 'You do know that you are very precious to me, don't you? I was devastated at the thought that I might have lost you.'

'I … I'm glad to hear it. I was distraught myself when I thought I may never see you again.'

'Does that mean you might come to love me eventually, do you think?'

Ianthe blinked and blurted out, 'Of course. I mean, I already do.' She felt her cheeks catch fire, realising what she had said. 'But please don't feel you have to reciprocate. I know you only married me because you need an heir and…'

'Ianthe, you goose, how could you possibly think that? I've adored you from the moment I set eyes on you at Almacks.'

'What? But you can't have done.'

'Oh, yes, I can. And I do. I only wish you were well enough so that I could prove it to you.'

Ianthe smiled, her heart doing little somersaults of happiness inside her chest. 'I'm absolutely fine and I order you to prove it immediately. You did say I was allowed to rule the roost in this house, did you not?'

He nodded with a grin. 'Within reason, of course, and as long as I agree with your decisions.'

'Well, then, you're not leaving this room until I'm entirely satisfied that you love me as much as I love you.'

He chuckled and pulled her into his embrace. 'It would seem I've found myself a somewhat bossy wife, but I think that is one order I'll happily comply with. Anything else, my lady?'

'No, Jason.' She sighed happily. 'Now I have absolutely everything that I have ever wished for.'

'As I do, my love.'

The publishers hope that this book has given you enjoyable reading. Large Print Books are especially designed to be as easy to see and hold as possible. If you wish a complete list of our books please ask at your local library or write directly to:

Dales Large Print Books
Magna House, Long Preston,
Skipton, North Yorkshire.
BD23 4ND